The Second Escape of Arthur Cooper

Cynthia M. Stowe

MARSHALL CAVENDISH · NEW YORK

Acknowledgements

I would like to thank the following people:

Louise Minks for getting me interested in writing historical fiction.

Hobson Woodward for giving me the true facts of the story of Arthur and Mary Cooper, and for his generous sharing of information.

My critique group members: Michael Daley, Jessie Haas, Jean Shaw and Nancy Hope Wilson for giving me suggestions on the story and for their constant support.

My agent Liza Voges for believing in me and in my writing.

Marshall Cavendish, 99 White Plains Road, Tarrytown, NY 10591

Library of Congress Cataloging-in-Publication Data
Stowe, Cynthia.
The second escape of Arthur Cooper / Cynthia M. Stowe.
   p.   cm.
Summary: in 1822, on Nantucket Island runaway slave Arthur Cooper and his family are protected from slave catchers by a family of Quakers.
ISBN 0-7614-5069-6
1.Cooper, Arthur, b. 1789–Juvenile fiction. [1. Cooper, Arthur, b. 1789–Fiction.
2. Fugitive slaves–Fiction. 3. Slaves–Fiction. 4. Quakers–Fiction. 5. Nantucket Island (Mass.)–Fiction.]. I. Title.
PZ7.S8915   Se   2000
[Fic]–dc21   99-057276

The text of this book is set in 12 point Berthold Baskerville.
Book design by Constance Ftera
Printed in the United States of America
First edition

6   5   4   3   2   1

To Robert

One

"Obediah! Obediah!"

Lydia and I heard Anna Macy calling from her roof walk as we hiked up the steep little hill to our house.

"She's up there again," Lydia said.

"She and Mama were good friends," I said. "Before Mama got hurt." Now, everything was either before Mama got hurt or after Mama got hurt. It was as if the whole world changed at that very moment when the horse got spooked and dumped Mama onto the hard ground. "I'll go up and bring her down." I leaned the bolt of cotton I was carrying against our front stairs.

"Be careful, Phebe. The fog looks really thick up there. Keep back from the railing, and don't stay up there too long. It's cold."

"Obediah! Obediah!"

"He's only been gone whaling a year," Lydia said. "He's not due back for two more."

"Mama says she misses him."

"She should be like the other women. They don't go calling for their husbands like fools in the fog."

"Mama says we shouldn't judge anyone else's sadness."

Lydia hugged herself. "I'm sick of sadness."

The stairs leading to the roof walk were in the back of

the Macys' house, so I opened their front door and headed down the long, dark, deserted hallway. Mistress Macy didn't have any children. Perhaps that was why she missed her husband so very much.

I started climbing slowly. It had been a long day. Up at five to fetch wood for the new cook stove, then sweep the kitchen, then help Lydia serve oatmeal to Papa and then to Mama, then eat myself. Then to school. The numbers and the letters hadn't made sense today. Not that they ever did.

I climbed. I liked to climb. I liked how my heart started racing, pumping loud inside me. I started climbing faster to see if I could make it get louder.

But I was nearing the top. The door was ajar, and I looked out.

She was holding onto the railing and leaning far over the edge. Would she fall off the roof if I startled her? Perhaps I should run quickly toward her and grab her fast.

No, there wouldn't be time.

I turned around and started quietly back down the stairs. At the foot of the first landing, I came back up again, stomping my feet and calling, "Mistress Macy! Mistress Macy! It's Phebe. Phebe Folger."

"Phebe? Is it thee?" At least she was turned toward the doorway and no longer leaning over the edge. "Come see," she said. "I see her approaching the harbor. I see the masts: full sails, all hands on board. All safe."

I couldn't see five feet in front of me, the fog was so

thick. Whatever Mistress Macy was seeing, I didn't think it was the *Essex* coming home.

"Come back down with me, Mistress Macy," I said.

"I see the ship. I do, Phebe. And last night, I had a dream that all hands were well. I did, Phebe."

"Please come down with me."

"He's coming home. They found hundreds of whales off Rhode Island. They did, Phebe. And they filled up with oil, and now they're coming home. That was my dream."

"But Mistress Macy—"

"And I think I saw . . . if this fog would just lift, I could see the masts. The sails were full." She was leaning far over the railing again.

I slowly came up beside her, and she grasped my hand. Her fingers were freezing, and she was shivering. "Look, look, Phebe. Does thee see her?" Her voice was high-pitched.

I felt the moist cold of the late March afternoon and heard the foghorns warning ships off the shore. I could barely see the roof of our house next door. When Papa and I went up to our roof walk on clear days when a ship really was approaching the harbor, we often looked over and saw Mistress Macy here in this very spot. I knew where my house was, but the fog had swallowed it. We were standing in an island of wet gray, where all colors and shapes had escaped into the mist. We were completely alone.

"Does thee see her? Does thee?" She was almost crying.

What would she do if I said no? She put her arm around my waist and pulled me close. She was so strong.

"Mistress Macy," I said. "Please, thee is hurting me."

"Oh, Phebe, I . . . I am sorry." She let me go.

"Please come down with me, Mistress Macy," I said.

"But I see him."

"Maybe we should go to the harbor and . . . I'll go with thee."

"No." She was crying now. "I have to be sure it's the *Essex*. I have to see her again."

"We can go ask my papa."

"Thee go," she said. "Look, thee is cold. I'll just stay here, until I . . . until . . . ."

Until she "saw" a ship's mast that wasn't there? Until she got so cold, she got sick?

"Mistress Macy," I said. I said it slowly and loud. "My mama needs thee. That's why I came up."

"Thy mama?"

"Yes, she's been asking for thee."

She stepped toward me away from the railing. "Is she better, thy mama? She must be better if she is asking for me."

I edged toward the door and held out my arm to her. My hand faded into the fog.

She came toward me a little.

"Please hurry. She wants to ask thee a very important question."

"What question?"

"I don't know. She just sent me up here to fetch thee. She says she needs thee."

"Well, I must. . . ."

"Can we go to her now? She says it's very important."

"If thy mama needs me, I will go. Now, back away from that side edge, Phebe. It's dangerous. Come quickly, now." She took my hand again and led me toward the stairway and down the steps.

Everything was fine now, I thought. Everything was just fine. Until Mistress Macy found out that Mama hadn't really asked for her, and Mama found out that I had lied.

Two

"Anna!" Mama was lying on her side. She rose up on her elbow when we came to her bedroom doorway.

"What is it, Katherine?" Mistress Macy said. "What does thee need to ask me?"

"Anna, I don't understand."

"I found her on the roof walk," I said, quickly sliding into the room.

"I saw the *Essex*, Katherine. I did. Obediah is coming home."

I lifted the quilt that was bunched up at Mama's feet and pulled it up over her shoulders. "It's cold," I said. "It's very cold today. And damp. I told Mistress Macy that–"

"Katherine, what did thee need to ask me? I need to get back. I have to make sure it's the *Essex* coming home."

"Anna, it seems too soon for Obediah to be–"

"Mama, look. Look how foggy it is today."

Mama turned her head to look out the window, completely gray now with the fog. "Ah."

"I told Mistress Macy thee needed to ask her something," I said.

"Ah. Well, Anna, I wanted to ask thee if . . . actually,

Phebe got it a little wrong. I really wanted to tell thee something."

"Is it important, Katherine? I need to get back."

"Wouldn't it be better to wait a few minutes, Anna? The fog will lift in a few minutes, I'm sure, and then thee can see better."

Mama winced.

"Does it hurt, Mama?"

"Yes, Phebe."

"Can I help thee, Katherine?"

"Yes, please, Anna. Please pull that chair over and come sit by me. This won't take long, and it would comfort me so to have thee visit for a few minutes. I've missed thee, Anna."

Mistress Macy hesitated, but then pulled a chair away from the wall and carried it over to Mama's bedside. I did the same.

"I can stay for a few minutes," she said.

Mama turned on her back and let her hands rest on her stomach. Her hands: They were so thin, so pale with the veins showing purple. They used to be so strong and tanned from working in the kitchen garden and cooking at the hearth.

"Well," Mama said. "Now, Lydia hasn't heard this news either, so thee both will be the first to know. Mary Cooper is coming to work for us."

"Is she Arthur Cooper's wife?" Mistress Macy asked.

"Yes, Abigail Pollard recommended her, and this means that Lydia can go back to school."

My stomach twisted. "Lydia will like that."

"But aren't there slave catchers in New Bedford?" Mistress Macy asked.

"Thee has heard it?"

"Yes, at thy husband's store this morning, when I went to get my molasses."

"But Mary is free-born," Mama said.

"Arthur escaped from Virginia. It's been a few years now. And their children—"

"The children follow the mother," I said. "I heard Papa talking. If the mother is free-born, the children are, too."

"I forget how much thee hears, Phebe." Mama smiled.

"Who saw the slave catchers?" I asked. "Who are they looking for?"

"Hush, now, Phebe," Mama said. "Let's not worry. It's probably just a rumor. I'll ask thy papa tonight. Mary will be here tomorrow, and Lydia will be able to go back to being a girl and not a nurse for her mother."

"She likes taking care of thee, Mama. I do too."

"And thee both do a fine job." She adjusted her pillow. "But, Anna, thee looks well."

Mistress Macy tucked back wisps of silvery light brown hair that had escaped the sides of her bonnet. "Now, thee tells a falsehood," she said. "I've lost so much weight. Obediah likes it when I'm carrying weight. He'll be unhappy when he gets home."

"I think thee is beautiful," I said. I did, too. In spite of her plain Quaker dress and dark bonnet, she had a pleasing form and a lovely, delicate face.

"Thee does lie, Phebe Folger," Mistress Macy said.

I felt hot. When I'd lied the first time, she hadn't found out about it, but now, when I'd told the truth . . . "I didn't lie."

"Is thee looking forward to the nice spring weather, Anna?" Mama asked.

"I'm old and ugly," Mistress Macy said.

"Thee is beautiful," I said. "Lydia even said so last First Day after Meeting. She was saying that—"

"Anna." Mama patted the bed. "Tell me about thyself. I haven't seen thee for so long."

"Oh, I clean that big house, and I cook my meals. Katherine, does thee remember when we used to see each other every afternoon?"

"Oh, I do. Tea and a biscuit and some talk over our sewing."

"Lots of talk over sewing," I said.

Mama laughed.

"What does the doctor say?" Mistress Macy suddenly stiffened in her chair. "Oh, I shouldn't have asked."

"No, that is fine, and it reminds me. Now I remember what it is I sent Phebe to ask thee. I don't know where my mind has been lately."

"It's natural. Thee has been sick."

"Well, Anna, the last time I saw Dr. Stackpole . . . I can have visitors, just one at first, and then we'll see."

"Mama." I jumped up and my chair clattered back onto the floor. "Thee is better."

"Let me finish," Mama said. "And I want to ask thee,

Anna, if thee will visit me every afternoon, for just a short while in the beginning."

Mistress Macy didn't answer. I stood and watched her and then looked even closer and saw that she was crying.

"Thee wants me to be thy visitor?"

"I do."

"Thee can have only one visitor, and thee wants it to be me?"

"Yes."

"I will. I will. I will be so happy to do that." She stood up. "I'll be here tomorrow. Now, I've got to go start the supper, and perhaps I'll make some muffins. Yes, Katherine, I will bring muffins for our tea tomorrow afternoon. Blueberry muffins, or perhaps some hickory nut muffins." She walked quickly through the doorway and down the stairs. We heard the door close.

"She'll be all right now," Mama said.

"Mama, thee is better."

She didn't answer.

"Mama?"

"Well, Phebe, thee is not the only person who told a lie today. Dr. Stackpole did not tell me that I could have visitors."

"But thee told—"

"I had to tell her that. She's up on the roof walk, in this fog, looking for her husband? I am lying hurt in this bed, but she is dying of loneliness. Having Anna visit me for a little while every afternoon will not hurt me."

"Thee needs thy rest."

"That's what Dr. Stackpole keeps telling me. But I'm starting to think I need other things as well."

I picked up my fallen chair and placed it back against the wall. I felt like crying. Mama wasn't any better, and. . . . "I'm sorry I lied, Mama. About thee needing her."

"Did thee tell the lie to help her?"

"Yes."

"Then God will forgive thee. And I will, too. We just won't mention this to Lydia or thy father."

Three

The next day it was raining gently but steadily when I got out of school and I lifted my face and let the raindrops cool me. Lydia was staying late at school today to help Master Gibbs. Papa had sent her back early this morning, saying that Mary Cooper would clean up the breakfast kitchen as soon as she arrived.

I quickened my steps. What would Mary be like? Would she be bossy, like Lydia?

It wasn't that Lydia was mean to me at school. It was just that she always looked so disappointed when she was helping in my class and I stumbled over the littlest words or couldn't remember my number facts. Lydia wanted her little sister to be smart, but all the school brains in the family had gone into Lydia's head.

I hurried faster. Would Mary be nice? Would she like me? We'd never before had someone working in our home.

The rain was lessening, but my heavy woolen cloak was soaking through, and my shoes and socks were wet. Oh, why not, since I was wet already: I stomped into a puddle in the sand street and felt the water splash around me. I stomped again and again and watched the water spray play with the raindrops.

"Phebe Folger!"

"Mistress Coffin!"

She stood squarely in front of me, not two feet away, her short, wide self blocking my path.

"And does thy papa know that thee is splashing like a baby in the street? I seem to recall that he had to pay Mistress Thomas to sew thee a dress last December because thy mother is sick. Perhaps it is this very dress you are splashing."

Why didn't Mistress Coffin mind her own business?

"My mother is getting better," I said. "She'll be able to sew my dresses very soon."

"Does thee speak to thy elders in that tone?"

"I'm . . . I'm sorry, Mistress Coffin. I did not mean to be disrespectful."

"Well, then."

"And I know I shouldn't have been splashing."

"Is thy mother really better?"

"Yes." There it was again: another lie. It was getting easier to tell them.

"Well, Phebe. We have all missed thy mother since she's been gone."

"I know, I . . . I have to go now, Mistress Coffin."

"Run along now, and give my best to thy mother. Since she's better, perhaps I can visit her one of these days."

I pretended I didn't hear the last part. If I didn't stop lying, I was going to get into a lot of trouble. Perhaps Mistress Coffin would forget about visiting.

But, perhaps, she wouldn't. I ran the rest of the way home.

Our big red house stood silent. All of the windows were closed against the rain, and the house rose high and dark on its steep little hill.

Maybe Mary wouldn't like me. Maybe she'd think I was a foolish little girl who couldn't learn her lessons.

I climbed the back steps and opened the door a crack. A delicious smell met me. Muffins? A cake? Maybe a sweet bread made with flour and eggs and lots of raisins like Mama used to make?

Mary was singing. Her back was to me as I stepped into the kitchen doorway. She was bending over, putting a piece of wood into the cook stove.

"Rock of ages, Let me be. Sweet my soul I come to thee."

Her voice was rich and smooth, like newly churned butter. She turned toward the hearth, and I watched as she pushed the wooden spatula into the side oven and drew out a loaf of bread.

She was tall and thin, slight of build, the color of molasses. She wore a green turban on her head and a dress made from a yellow, red, and orange print. She carried herself so tall and proud.

Mary wasn't going to like a silly girl like me.

She turned and saw me. "Hello. You must be Phebe."

I nodded.

"You're wet."

I nodded.

"Goodness, child. You are soaked through. Take off that cloak and those shoes and socks, and let's dry them by the fire. How in heaven's name did you get so wet?"

"Well, I . . ." I wasn't going to lie this time. But before I could answer, there was a loud crash. And then a wail. I turned to see a little boy in the back corner of the kitchen. He was sitting in the middle of a broken crockery of blackberry jam, with jam all over his face and hands.

"Robert!" Mary ran and snatched the little boy up into her arms. "Hush. Hush now. Are you cut?"

He howled.

Mary set him down on the side table and felt all over his face and hands. "It doesn't look like he's cut. No, I don't see anything, and there's no blood. Thanks be. But the crock is broken, and all that jam."

"It was an accident. Here, I'll wash him so we can see better." I raised the wet rag I'd gotten toward the baby, but then stopped.

"Thank you," Mary took the rag and wiped off Robert's face. "Hush now, be still. You're all right. There's no need to cry." She turned the baby toward me. "Here. You wash his hands. I'm sure he's all right."

I took one of his plump little hands and washed each of his fingers. His skin was so soft, his hands so round and fat. He tried to pull away, but I held on. "It's all right," I told him. "I'm helping thee." The color of his skin was so beautiful: a darker shade of brown than his mother's, lighter on the palm.

He stopped crying and stared at me with dark, soft eyes. I rested for a moment and stared back. He was such a solid little boy, with lots of baby fat. I'm small and skinny. Papa always says they have to hold on to me in windstorms so that the wind won't carry me away into the ocean.

"I'll have to pay for the crock with my first pay," Mary said. "What will your parents think of me, to break something valuable on my first day?"

"It was an accident."

"I never should have left him alone near that crock. I should have known better."

"Papa says that accidents happen."

"But, it was my mistake, and I should pay for it."

"I'll tell then I did it. They won't get angry at me."

Mary stopped short. "Phebe, no. It's thoughtful of you, kind . . . but, I'll tell your mama this afternoon."

"Mama won't get angry," I said.

Robert stayed quiet as I washed the last of the jam off his fingers. Then, he gurgled and smiled.

"I think this means you're friends," Mary said.

"How old is he?"

"Three, but young for his age. I spoil him because he's my baby."

"Does thee have other children?"

"Eliza Ann, she's twelve. Cyrus, he's nine, and Randolf, he's seven."

"Lydia's sixteen," I said. "I'm ten. I'm a year older than Cyrus."

"Thank you for helping with Robert," Mary said. "I shouldn't have left him alone with that jam."

"I'm glad he didn't get cut. He's sweet."

Mary laughed and lifted Robert up and hugged him. "Now that he's quiet, he's sweet." She kissed him and set him back down into a chair. "You sit there, please, and don't you get into any more trouble. I've got to clean up."

"I can help. I've got the rag."

Mary smiled. "I'll get another bucket of water from the well."

Four

"Was Arthur really a slave?" I asked. I was helping Mary peel potatoes for tonight's fish chowder. Robert was sleeping in our kindling box next to the hearth, snoring soft, little-boy snores. I'd taken out the sticks, and Mary had lined the box with our big brown blanket.

"Poor baby, he's so tired," Mary said.

"But was Arthur really a slave?" I asked.

"You do keep your teeth on a question, don't you, Miss Phebe." Mary reached over and patted my hand.

"I've never known a slave before. I mean, I know that thee were free-born, but . . . but Lydia says that slavery is horrible, and . . . I'm sorry. I'm probably asking too many questions."

"It is hard to speak of," Mary said. "Eliza Ann and Cyrus ask, too, and Arthur and I, we don't know how to speak of it."

"Thee could just tell us."

Mary laughed. "That is exactly what Eliza Ann says. But it's not for the ears of children."

We sat and peeled. I slid my knife under the thin brown skin of my potato, and then cut out a bad spot. When would Lydia get home? Why wasn't she coming home early to meet Mary?

"But was Arthur really a slave?"

Mary sighed. "You are just like my daughter." She placed another potato in the washing bowl and counted. "One, two, three, four, five, six, seven. Now listen, I've planned on putting ten potatoes in tonight's chowder. I'll tell you about Arthur for three more potatoes."

"A three-potato story. Good."

"Well, now." Mary put her hands in her lap and watched me. "And that doesn't mean you can slow down your peeling."

"I'm working fast. See?"

"Well, I'll tell you about Arthur's grandmother. He lived with Gram until he was five years old."

"Was she free-born?"

"Oh no, she was a slave her whole life. David Ricketts gave her freedom papers after she'd worked for them over seventy years. He gave her a shack in the woods and freedom papers—maybe he thought she could eat those. But Gram fooled them all."

"How?" All of a sudden I heard footsteps in the front hall, and then Lydia was standing right in front of us in the kitchen.

"Phebe, go fetch wood for tonight's fires," she said.

"But I'm helping Mary."

"Go get the wood."

"I'm peeling potatoes. I'll get the wood later."

"It's all right, Phebe," Mary said. "I can finish this up in just a few minutes."

"But—"

"Phebe, you're not supposed to bother Mary."

"I'm not bothering her. I'm helping."

"It's nice to meet you, Miss Lydia," Mary said. "I'll leave the fish chowder on a low fire in the hearth so that when I go home you can serve it to your mother and father."

"Thee is supposed to use the new cook stove."

"Your father said something about that, but I'll be danged if I can figure out how to use the thing."

"The cook stove saves wood."

"The cook stove will burn your supper if I don't first learn how to use it."

Lydia stared at Mary, but Mary just kept on with her peeling. She began to softly hum the same song I'd heard her sing when I first came into the kitchen.

It seemed as if Lydia didn't know what to do with her hands. First, she put them on her hips, and then she clasped them together, and then she let them fall by her side.

"Thee can finish the potatoes, Phebe. But do it quickly. And then go get the wood." Lydia turned and left the kitchen and went upstairs.

I sighed. "I'd better hurry. I know her, she'll be back in a few minutes."

Mary didn't answer, but at least she wasn't still humming.

"I'm sorry that my sister was rude to thee, Mary."

Mary sighed deeply and then looked up at me. "Your mama being sick is hard on her, on all of you, I would imagine. Come now, I had promised to tell you about Arthur's grandmother."

"Tell me fast, before Lydia gets back."

"Well, let's see now. Gram had been a baking cook at

the plantation, so when she got free, she just kept on making those delicious cakes and cookies. Arthur says that people used to line up at the outside door on Wednesdays to get one of her apple pies–it was pie-making day on Wednesdays."

"Did Arthur like her pies?"

"Did he! Try as I like, I can't make a pie as good as his grandmother's."

I heard footsteps overhead, loud stomps. Lydia was stomping her feet.

"But why did Arthur run away if Gram was–"

Mary tossed her potato into the cleaning bowl and stood up quickly. "You'd better go get that wood," she said, "and I'd better check on my boy."

"But why did Arthur . . . ."

But Mary was already bending over the kindling box and lifting up Robert. He leaned against his mother in his sleep and snuggled against her. She hugged him. "So sweet when he's sleeping," she said.

"I thank thee for telling me about Arthur's grandmother." I placed my last potato in the bowl and stood up.

"You are most welcome, Miss Phebe."

I turned back at the doorway and watched Mary swaying back and forth with Robert in her arms, singing softly to him. Mary wasn't telling me the whole story. Mary had only told me a nice story about Arthur's Gram.

How did Arthur get taken from his grandmother? How did he get sent into slavery? And why and how did he run away?

Five

Papa brought me home a new drawing book from the store. It was so wonderful: it had a marbled cover with many pages. The cover was so beautiful, I thought maybe it was a sin because we're not supposed to like things of this world. But Papa says that the browns are of God's good earth and the golds are of the sands. God made those colors, so they cannot be evil. And Papa brought me home a new quill pen and a bottle of ink. He said it was not a present. It was something I needed.

"It's not a drawing book, it's a diary," Lydia said. "She shouldn't use it until she can write. It's a sin to use it for pictures."

"Pictures are Phebe's way of writing right now," Papa said.

"She has to work harder to learn her letters."

"I work hard," I said.

Lydia sat down next to me and took my hand. "I know thee does, Phebe, sometimes. But I watched thee at school today. Thee spent a lot of time looking out the window."

I shrugged. I tried to pay attention to my letters, but they were all so confusing, always changing shape every time I looked at them. It made me happy to look away from them and to watch the March wind play with the branches. Why exactly did the wind blow? It had something to do with the temperature.

"Make us a drawing, Phebe," Papa said.

I picked up my new bottle of ink, opened it and poised it over my inkwell. "I'll wait until later," I said. I ran upstairs and put the new drawing book under my bed.

*   *   *

We were in Mama's room after our supper. Mama's food tray was on a chair next to her bed, sitting there with a full bowl of fish chowder, a piece of bread and an apple. "How did thee like being back at school today, Lydia?" Mama asked.

"I liked it. Master Gibbs had me listen to the older children's geography lesson. Mama, Master Gibbs says that it's not right that there's no school for the other people on the island."

Papa was standing, looking out the window. He turned. "They could make their own, like we do."

"Schools cost money," Lydia said. "The Negro people and the Portuguese and the people from the South Sea Islands–they don't have a lot of money. The schools should be free, like in the rest of Massachusetts."

"We're not known for wanting to be like anyone else," Papa said.

"Quakers of the Nation of Nantucket," Mama said.

Lydia picked up Mama's tray and placed it next to her on the bed. "Eat some fish chowder," she said. "The Elders just want to save money. That's why they don't want the free school for everyone."

"Lydia!" Mama almost raised her voice. But then she picked up her piece of bread and took a bite.

"Lydia, I worry that thee has too many opinions for a girl," Papa said.

"Mama always says what she thinks," I said.

"But this is our home," Papa said. "A young woman needs to look and act—"

"Dutiful?" Mama asked.

"Soft-spoken," Papa said.

Mama chewed. Papa watched. He laughed.

"Well, an argument seems good for thy mother, Lydia," he said, "so I won't scold thee. But keep thy opinions of thy Elders within these walls."

"Mary's daughter Eliza Ann goes to school," I said. "Mary told me."

"The Zion Methodist Church just started one," Lydia said. "That's what I mean. They shouldn't have to. People in that church don't have a lot of money."

"Why does thee care about that?" I asked.

"I care about people."

"But thee was rude to Mary."

"Lydia!" Mama did raise her voice this time.

"I was not rude to Mary," Lydia said. "I just asked her to use the new cook stove."

"Thee was rude."

"I was not."

"Girls!" Papa stood up and walked over to the fireplace. He stared down at the embers and then turned. "Lydia, was thee rude to Mary?"

"No, Papa."

Yes, Papa, I thought. Lydia was lying. Even my perfect sister lied sometimes. "Mary told me that Arthur lived with his grandmother until he was five," I said. Why had I said that? Sometimes, words just escaped from my mouth without my even thinking.

"Phebe was bothering Mary," Lydia said.

"That is enough." Papa came back and sat by Mama's bedside. "Let's have no more talk of who did what."

"Arthur was a sick little boy, and the master at the plantation, this David Ricketts, thought he would die, so he sent him to his grandmother because he didn't want to feed a sick child," Lydia said.

"How does thee know?"

"And then his grandmother took good care of him, and he got healthy and fat, so they brought him back to the plantation when he was five."

"How does thee know?" I asked.

Lydia smiled. "Anna Gardner told me because Arthur built a porch for her father, and he talked about his escape one morning."

"How did Arthur escape?"

"Anna doesn't know. That's all her father would tell her."

Was Lydia lying again? Did she know how Arthur had escaped? I watched her. She reached over and picked up the bowl of chowder and handed Mama the spoon.

Lydia might know more. But, tonight, she wasn't saying.

Six

It was a perfect day, with blue sky and puffy clouds, a day that could make me forget the wet fog that so often covered our island.

"Look, Mama," I said, opening the window. "It's spring."

"It's spring for today," she said. "Thee knows what April is like. Today, it's beautiful, and tomorrow, we'll have an ice storm. But hurry on thy way, Phebe. Mary and Arthur will be waiting for thee."

We were going to the dock where Arthur was going to barter sacks of peat from the marsh for lumber. I should have been hurrying, but on this sunny Saturday morning, I hated leaving Mama. "What will thee do today?" I asked.

Mama smiled a soft, little smile. "I'll do what I've been doing these last seven months: lie in bed and try to rest."

I looked around Mama's bedroom. It had plain, simple walls, like all of our rooms. Lydia had placed two of my drawings against the blanket chest: the one of the harbor and the one of Wigwam Pond. Lydia said that it was all right to have them in the room, because it wasn't decorating. Drawing was my gift from God, and Mama needed something to remind her of the beauty of God's island.

"But, Mama, thee used to be so busy."

"I know, Phebe. And we used to take long, lovely walks on days like this. Lovely, long walks when we should have been cooking or cleaning or helping thy Papa in the store."

"Papa didn't mind."

"I know. Does thee remember our walks, Phebe?"

I came and sat next to her on the bed. "We used to walk quickly through town, so that everyone would think we were on an errand."

"Keep our heads high and look straight ahead."

"Up past the windmills and past Angola Street."

"And when we reached the town gate, we'd open it and slip out fast."

"And once we were past No Bottom Pond, we knew we were safe; no one would see us."

"Only the sheep. And maybe the peat diggers."

"And the rabbits, and the meadow birds. Remember the snake we saw in the marsh, Mama?"

She laughed. "I will never forget it. That young fellow had to be six feet long."

"Sunning himself on a rock."

I used to love walking with Mama. We didn't do it very often, but once in awhile, she would call to me from the kitchen, and when I got there, she'd be taking her apron off and smiling. That would be the sign.

Sometimes, we walked to the Middle Meadow, and sometimes, especially on windy days, we walked all the way to the ocean's edge and watched the waves breaking on the rocks, furious with power.

But, today, Mama was lying in bed, pale and weak. When she turned or tried to move in bed, she looked like an injured seabird, flapping on the shore.

I was suddenly mad at Mama. "Why did thee have to take that ride in that carriage?" I covered my mouth. I was almost yelling.

Mama just lay there. Finally, she said, "Many's the time I've asked myself that same question." She took my hand and raised it to her lips and kissed it. "Thee run along now, Phebe. Arthur and Mary will be waiting for thee."

I ran all the way to Arthur and Mary's. It wasn't far. Our house was on India Street, so all I had to do was run up Center to Main and then go across Pleasant, climb the steep hill to the three windmills, and then go on to Angola Street.

All the houses on the street were close together, with little yards in front and wooden gates blocking off secret pathways to the back. Arthur and Mary's was a pretty white cottage near the corner. It was so much smaller than ours. Our house reached two stories, and then we had the roof and the roof walk. On Angola Street, I could see all of Mary's cottage in one quick glance.

She opened the door to my knock. "Phebe, come in and meet my family."

My feet, which had tripped so lightly over the sand streets to get here, suddenly felt heavy.

"Come, now," Mary said. "Everyone wants to meet you."

The skinniest girl I ever saw sat on the one wooden chair in the parlor. There was a bench along the far wall, and on that sat one boy older than I and another who was much younger. The big boy lifted his hands as if to wave, and then he smiled. All three of them stared at me. The younger boy took his brother's hand.

"Now, you must be Phebe," a voice said. A tall man with a kind, serious face came into the parlor. His hair was cut short to his head, graying and curly. He was holding Robert.

Robert reached his arms out toward me and struggled to get down. "Phebe. Phebe." He ran to me, and I snatched him up and held on to him hard.

"Is it all right if Robert walks with you?" Mary asked. "I want Eliza Ann and the boys to carry these sacks."

Suddenly, the room was in motion, like the waves rushing in and swirling around big boulders on the shore.

"I can carry the biggest one, Mother," Eliza Ann said.

"No, me," Cyrus said.

"I'm the strongest." It was Eliza Ann. How could she be strong? She was like a swamp grass, so tall and skinny.

Mary laughed. "Let's see who's claiming to be strongest halfway to the wharf. Come on, now. I'll decide who carries what, and let's have no more arguing."

Seven

It was hard to keep up. Arthur was taking long, loose strides, his legs swinging forever forward. Mary and the boys were half running, and Eliza Ann was half dragging her enormous sack on the ground. Mary *had* given her the biggest one.

"Is the ship already docked?" Mary asked.

"It came in yesterday's late light," Arthur answered. "We'll get the best choice of lumber if we get there early."

I was sorry that I had agreed to walk with Robert. He was moving as quickly as he could, but his little legs couldn't carry him fast enough. He held on to my hand with all his strength, and I struggled to pull along the forty pound little-boy anchor that felt tied to my body.

Robert began to cry.

"What's this?" Arthur stopped, turned, and then came back to the end of the line to Robert and me. "Is my little boy unhappy?" He scooped up his son and held him up to the sky. Then he brought him close and kissed him.

Arthur seemed to sense me watching him. "Have I been running?" he asked.

I nodded.

He laughed. "I'm sorry. I'll slow down." Arthur lifted Robert onto his shoulders.

"Where is the new room going to be?" I asked, falling into step beside Mary.

"On the side of the kitchen. Arthur is going to close in the porch."

"Will it be for the new baby?" Mary had told me that a new baby was due in October.

"No. We'll give it to Eliza. I don't want the baby that far away from me at night."

"And Eliza Ann will sleep there, away from the boys," Arthur said.

"It will be a small room," Mary said.

"The whole house is small."

Mary laughed. "Big enough."

"Big enough," he agreed. He took a few steps. "I'm putting in a glass window."

"We can afford it?"

"It will be small." This time, they both laughed.

"But big enough," they said.

* * *

The deep oily smell was the first thing that told me we were nearing the harbor. I didn't hate it like Lydia did, making her face tight and holding her nose whenever we walked downtown. The smell was whale oil, and Papa always said that if it weren't for whale oil, people wouldn't have the money to spend at our store. So I decided to like the smell, even though sometimes, when the wind carried it a little farther out past the harbor than I expected, the strength of it surprised me and made me stop my breath.

We walked past the big white Congregational church with the tall steeple. It was set back from the road, with meadow grass out front. Two sheep grazed there. I hoped that Papa would let me go to the shearing festival this May. It was a favorite day for me, watching the sheep getting their warm wool cut off for the summer.

"You're quiet today, Miss Phebe," Mary was smiling. "Why don't you help Eliza Ann carry that sack?"

Eliza Ann stopped short and watched me.

"I'll help," I said. "But only if she wants me to."

Eliza Ann stood silent.

"If we carry it together," I said, "we can beat the boys to the harbor."

A slow smile spread across Eliza Ann's face. "Here," she said. "You take this end. We'll march like the British soldiers did in the war. I'll be the captain. You listen to me, so we can do it together. Here, now: left, right, left, right, left. Left, right, left, right, left."

It was working. We were speeding ahead of the others. Cyrus and Randolf tried to catch up, but we were twenty feet ahead of them by the time we reached the Town Hall.

"Hello, you two," Arthur called. "Slow down."

"Left, right, left, right, left," I called. Then, we both started laughing so hard we dropped the sack and rolled on the ground.

* * *

The whaling ships were so beautiful, with all their masts reaching up into the bright blue sky. We walked toward the *Industry* and the *Loper.* I raised my head and looked farther out over the harbor past the three long docks. I saw a great flock of ships. Papa says that Nantucket sailors travel to every port in the world.

There were people everywhere, people of all colors and sizes. Papa says that we're lucky to live on an island that the world comes to visit, that we can see and know people of every country who come in on the whaling and trade ships. Papa says that people who live on the mainland get to meet only a few different types of people, maybe some freed Negro slaves or even a few Indians. Papa says that meeting all these people makes people on Nantucket more knowing and wiser about the world.

But until I met Mary and her family, I'd never really known a Negro person, not to speak with or to know.

As we reached the wharves, people jostled us with their comings and goings: sailors carrying large wooden boxes or big canvas sacks, women grabbing children back as they tried to run toward the water.

A group of Quaker men stood near the beginning of the biggest dock, their long, somber coats waving slightly in the breeze. As soon as they saw us, they stopped talking. Finally, Gilbert Coffin walked over.

"Arthur," he said. "I need to speak with thee."

"What is wrong?" Arthur asked. "You act as if something is wrong."

"Why doesn't thee leave thy family here and–"

"No." Mary walked to Arthur's side, took his hand and faced the men.

Arthur nodded. "I keep no secrets from my family."

Gilbert Coffin looked over to the other Quaker men who now stood as still as statues. He stared at some sailors who were coiling rope into huge rough circles. And then he turned back to Arthur. "Master Starbuck, the captain of the *Hero*, brings word that slave catchers have been spotted in New Bedford."

Mary stiffened tall, her whole body becoming rigid.

Arthur cradled Robert close. "Do you know anything of these men?" he asked.

"There are three of them asking questions in New Bedford. They are asking about several people. Thy name was mentioned."

Arthur put his free arm around Mary. "Thank you for telling us," he said. "I greatly appreciate the information. It will give us time to make plans."

Eight

Everything itched: my shoulder and my nose and the back of my head. Lydia turned and scowled at me.

I know I told her with my eyes. I know I'm supposed to be quiet at Meeting.

Quiet and still. Absolutely quiet. Maybe I'd stop breathing and die, and then she'd be sorry.

I looked up at the Elders who sat facing us on their long wooden bench. Most of them sat with their heads bowed. Quiet and still. They sat as stonelike as cliffs by the sea.

Gilbert Coffin twitched in his seat. Maybe he had a message to tell us. That would be good. Whenever Gilbert Coffin spoke in Meeting, he talked for a long time, and that made the time go by faster.

But then Gilbert Coffin shook a little, the movement dying in his heavy, dark cloak and trousers. And then he was silent.

I knew that I was supposed to be thinking about God, waiting for God to send me wisdom. But on this chilly First Day morning, God seemed very far away from our windswept island. How could God let slave catchers come to New Bedford? How could God let slavery exist? And why weren't we doing something? Why were the

Elders just sitting there, not moving, not even breathing, it seemed. Why weren't they over there in New Bedford getting rid of those slave catchers?

It was not the Quaker way. Papa says that we do no violence against any man.

I looked up at Papa. He was sitting between Tristam Paddock and Thomas Mitchell, his head bowed like the others. He must have felt me looking at him because his head rose, and he glanced in my direction.

Lydia poked me. I poked her back. I stared straight ahead. I'd be so quiet. I'd be quieter than Lydia, and for longer. Lydia would sneeze or cough or maybe she'd fall asleep and snore, and then I would have to poke her again in the side and give her a stern look. And I would have to poke her hard.

Those slave catchers wanted to do violence against Arthur. They wanted to take him back and make him be a slave again for that Mr. Ricketts. And there were many stories about how they beat slaves who were returned. They beat them and locked them up, and. . . .

My fists tightened. Meeting was taking forever. I made pleats in my skirt, but the fabric was heavy and coarse, and the pleats were ugly, not at all like the tiny delicate ones I'd sewn yesterday afternoon when we'd all gotten back to the cottage from the wharf. I had stayed and helped Mary sew sleeping garments for the new baby. My fabric was soft and pretty: a robin's-egg blue with tiny purple violets and pansies. I'd been so careful to get all the pleats just right.

Eliza Ann and Mary and I had sat there, not speaking, just pushing our needles in and pulling them out. We worked as if the three of us could keep the slave catchers away if only we kept sewing.

We should do something. We should not just be sitting here in Meeting. Dressed in our dark heavy clothing, we looked like dried-out lumps of coal.

Gilbert Coffin stirred. And again. This time, he stood up. "Friends," he said. "I have sat for all of Meeting now, trying to think about God." He stood silent. "But all I can think about," he went on, "is the look on Arthur Cooper's face when I told him that he and his family are in danger. I see the look on his dear wife's face, and the fear on the faces of their children. One of our own—he nodded to me—stood with them. (I bolted upright in my seat.) We call ourselves the people of God, but what are we doing in the presence of this evil?

What is God's will? I ask myself. What does God require of me? Does God ask that I sit idly by while Arthur Cooper and his family carry this dreadful fear by themselves?"

He stood, not speaking for a long minute. "And, I know that I should be asking God for guidance, but all I can think of is vengeance and anger."

Gilbert Coffin was just like me!

"How dare slave catchers come and threaten this man: a good man, whose ancestors' lives were stolen from them by slavers years ago. My heart tells me we should fight them. I want to fight them."

Words of anger in Meeting? Even Lydia was staring at Gilbert Coffin.

"And then I heard God asking me one simple question. Why is it that when I first heard the news, my first response was to tell Arthur that he must make plans for his family? Why did I not tell him that I, that we, will make plans, that we will help him together, with God's help?"

No one moved. No one breathed, it seemed. It was completely silent.

"Friends," he said. "I propose a special meeting after worship. I ask all who are willing to join me."

Nine

I wanted to go to the meeting, but Lydia said I had to help her at home, and Papa said that the meeting was not for children.

"Children help in the South," I said, "in the Underground Railroad."

"That's true, Phebe, but in the South, it's necessary. There is no need for thee to endanger thyself here."

"I don't care about the danger, and I'd be good at helping. The slave catchers wouldn't suspect me."

Papa bent over and lifted up my chin. I could smell the wood smoke from the fire on his fingers.

"I know that thee wants to help thy friends, Phebe. And I promise, if there is something thee can do, I will ask."

"But Papa—"

"Go home now, Phebe."

"But Papa—"

He let go of my chin and stood tall. He breathed deeply and held his lips together tightly.

"Yes, Papa."

"Phebe, hurry up," Lydia said. "Thee has to get the wood for Mama's fire. It's cold today and windy."

I turned and ran. I was so angry. It wasn't fair that I couldn't go to the meeting, just because I was a "child."

I ran, my feet pounding the sand street, my fists punching the air.

But Lydia was right about Mama. Last week, when we'd gotten home from Meeting, Mama had been shivering in bed. A log had fallen out of her fireplace, and the room was cold. But if that log had been burning, Mama could have been trapped in bed, watching her room catch fire.

I loosened my fists and ran faster. Because of the accident last week, I'd been building Mama's fires more carefully and smaller. And Lydia was right: today was damp and cold, and Mama could be freezing.

I was out of breath by the time I reached home. I ran up the granite steps leading to the back door and raced past the kitchen and up the steep winding stairway.

Mama was sitting up in bed!

"Mama, is thee all right? Thee is supposed to be lying down. Is it the fire? Is something wrong?"

The fire was still smouldering, and it was in its proper place. The room was only cool.

"Mama, lie down. What's wrong?"

"Nothing, Phebe. Come over here and sit by me."

"Mama, is thee better? Oh, that would be so wonderful, so–"

"Come, Phebe. Sit."

I didn't know what to do, but I lifted one of the wooden chairs from against the wall and placed it next to Mama's bed.

"Is thee better?"

"I don't know. I think, perhaps, I am."

"Does it hurt?" I asked.

"Yes. I got dizzy at first. But this morning, I got so upset about the slave catchers, and then I got angry that I was stuck in this bed and couldn't do anything, and then I just. . . . It was something Mary said. She'd brought us tea, and Anna asked about Arthur's escape. It was impolite, and Mary didn't seem to want to answer, but I think because it was Anna asking. . . . She said that Arthur first hid for three months in a tiny crawl space above his grandmother's toolshed. When it was finally time for him to go to the ship, he couldn't walk."

"Why?"

"He'd had to lie on his back the whole time, for three months. His muscles had frozen. They were searching everywhere for him; his grandmother's house, the attic, the shed. But they just didn't imagine someone being in such a tiny space. They just didn't see it."

"He couldn't walk?"

"No, he collapsed when he tried to come down. But the ship was docked for two weeks, and his grandmother rubbed his muscles back to life."

"Arthur hadn't fallen," Lydia said.

I jumped. My sister was at the top of the stairs. How had she come up so quietly?

"His back wasn't broken," Lydia said. "Mama, thee has to lie down."

"No, Lydia. I will die if I stay in this bed much longer. I'm not getting better."

"Thee has to lie down. Now."

"No. I have to try something. Maybe I'm just like Arthur. Maybe I just have to move."

* * *

We were in the kitchen making apple muffins.

"I'm going to tell Papa as soon as he gets home from the meeting," Lydia said. "He'll make her lie down."

"But maybe she shouldn't. Maybe–"

"And Arthur and Mary should go into hiding," Lydia said. "They should take the children and go to the Bahamas, or to Canada. Especially with the baby coming in October. They'll be safe there."

"No," I said. "They can hide here until the slave catchers go away. Then Mary can come back and take care of Mama. She's getting better with Mary here."

"No she's not," Lydia said. "They have to leave. They have to go away from here."

I suddenly wanted to throw the batter I was mixing into Lydia's face. "Thee just wants to get rid of them," I said. "Thee hates Mary." I was yelling.

"I do not." Lydia faced me, her fists in the air.

I didn't care. She could try to hit me if she wanted to. "Thee is bad to Mary," I yelled.

"She won't use the cook stove."

"She doesn't know how."

"And now she's got Mama sitting up in bed." Lydia picked up the muffin pan and threw it against the wall.

The crash made both of us jump. We stared at the pan lying quiet now on the floor.

46

"Mary didn't make Mama sit up."

"It was that story she told."

"She just told Mama about Arthur. Anna Macy asked her."

"And now Mama thinks that just because Arthur got better, she will, too."

"Maybe she will." My voice was getting louder again. "Maybe she won't."

"Girls!" Papa was entering the kitchen. "What is the matter? And what is the muffin pan doing on the floor?"

Silence surrounded us.

"Mama was sitting up in bed," Lydia said. "I tried to get her to lie down, but she wouldn't. She says that—"

But Papa was already leaving. He turned and raced up the stairs toward the bedroom.

*　　*　　*

Later that afternoon, just before dusk, when the sun was almost swallowed by the ocean, I went to Lydia's room. She was lying on her bed, face down. I think she'd been crying. I felt so tired, my arms and legs feeling heavy and slow. I knelt down beside her.

"I'm sorry I yelled," I said. "I'm sorry that I said that thee doesn't like Mary."

Lydia half-sat up and rubbed her eyes. "Everything is different now. Mama doesn't need me anymore. She doesn't depend on me."

"Yes, she does."

"Not as much."

"But I thought thee would like being able to go back to

school and help Master Gibbs. I thought thee liked being a teacher."

"I do. But does thee remember the day when Mama got hurt?"

I closed my eyes. I could still see Thomas Daggett carrying Mama into the house, her body limp, her face pale and frightened.

"I thought my life was ended," Lydia said. "I thought that Mama was going to die."

I nodded.

Lydia got up and sat on the side of the bed. She patted her blanket, and I sat next to her. "And then I started doing all the chores and getting up extra early and working hard, and it got so that I got used to Mama being in bed. She seemed all right. She was still Mama."

I leaned against my sister. She took my hand.

"But now," Lydia went on, "Mama's not doing what the doctor said. She's listening to Mary."

"Does thee think it's really bad for her?"

"Yes, I do. She's got to obey the doctor."

"Papa will talk to her. He'll get her to stay lying down."

"Does thee think he can make her?"

"Papa can do anything."

Lydia sighed and kissed my hand. "Thee is right," she said. "Papa can do anything."

*   *   *

Later that day, Papa told us they had made plans at the meeting.

"What plans?"

"There are some houses, some safe places," he said.

"But—"

"No more. It's better that only a few people know."

"But we won't tell."

"I made a promise, girls. Go back to thy sewing."

Ten

Nothing happened. April moved into May and then into June.

On clear days, Anna Macy still climbed to her roof walk and looked out to the sea, searching for her husband Obediah. Lydia and I went to school. The air turned warm and gentle, and flowers colored the ground. There was no more news of the slave catchers. They seemed to have left New Bedford, but no one knew where they had gone.

Mary didn't sing as she worked anymore. Most often, her beautiful face was set firm and unsmiling.

And Mama wasn't sitting up. Most days now, she lay quietly in bed. She was obeying Dr. Stackpole.

I went to school and stood day after day at the recitation bench, making mistakes with my reading.

One day, Lydia told me to stay after school. "Thee will learn, Phebe," she said. "I will help thee."

"But I want to go home to Mama," I said. "I'm tired."

"Mama wants thee to learn to read."

"But I can't."

"Thee is not stupid."

"I can't remember the letters."

Lydia picked up my slate and made a mark. "What letter is this?"

"A 'b'?"

"No, it's a 'd.' What about this?"

"A 't'?"

"That's right."

"But they don't stay the same. They change when I look at them."

Lydia stared at me. "But thee is a smart girl," she said. It was almost like she was talking to herself. "Thee learns how to do things I show thee at home." She walked to the door and stood looking out at the road, busy now with rattling carriages. "I'll just have to show thee the letters."

"But—"

"No, I'm not going to write them. I'm going to show them."

"How?"

"I don't know." Lydia picked up her knitting and started out the door. But then, she turned. "Phebe, do you remember how hard it was for you to learn to knit when Mama and I just told thee how to do it?"

I nodded. "And then Mama had me feel her fingers and the way it felt when she knitted."

"And thee learned. And now thee is an excellent knitter." Lydia pulled a scrap piece of yarn from her bag and twisted it into a circle. "Don't look at the letter," she told me. "Put thy finger on it and trace it, and then say its name. Then look at it. See it's an 'o.' Say 'o.'"

"O."

"Now, feel it again."

I closed my eyes this time. "O" I sighed. "I thank thee for trying to help me," I said, "but–"

"Go home," Lydia said. "But tomorrow, we'll really start working."

* * *

Mary wasn't in the kitchen when I got there.

"Eliza Ann was feeling poorly," Mama said. "Chicken pox, we think. And Mary's worried about Robert and the others, of course. So I told her to go home early."

"But thee is all alone."

"Only for a short while. Mary just left, and she has the supper stew already cooking."

"Mama, thee looks . . . ."

"What, Phebe?"

"Thee looks tired."

"I am tired, Phebe."

There was a sound downstairs, and I ran to open the door.

It was Dr. Stackpole. "Miss Phebe. And how is our little miss today?"

"Getting bigger," I said, "and older."

He laughed. "Thee is right. I'm sorry. I forget how fast thee grows." He smiled, his whole face softening into a happy round ball.

I remembered that I used to like Dr. Stackpole, before what he made Mama do made her so unhappy. Last year, before Mama got hurt, when I'd had a bad fever, he'd come and put cool cloths on my forehead. And he'd held my hand and told me a story about when he'd been young and afraid.

I got better from the fever, and Mama had said it was because of Dr. Stackpole.

"I'll see myself up," he told me.

I put a log on the kitchen fire, and then another. Then, I climbed halfway up the stairs, slowly and quietly, and sat on a middle step. I strained to hear.

"Sarah Coleman tells me that Anna Macy is visiting," Dr. Stackpole said.

I heard mumbling. I couldn't hear Mama's answer.

"I know that thee is trying to help her," he said, "but thee must think of thyself and thy husband and children."

More mumbling. I crept up two more steps.

"Thee must rest. I have consulted with a specialist in Boston. He agrees with my treatment."

"Anna comes and keeps me company," Mama said. "Yes, I'm happy if visiting me helps her, but I need her too. She brings me news and we talk. We're friends."

"If she was thy friend, she would be following my orders. She would be helping thee get better by letting thee rest."

"I rest twenty-four hours a day. I will die of rest."

"Katherine, it is wrong to speak like that. Thee must pray to God to give thee strength to endure this trial. I wrote a specialist in Boston, Katherine. He agrees with my treatment. Thee must rest."

Silence.

"I described your condition in detail."

Silence.

"Katherine, I'll come by to see thee again later this week."

Silence.

I crept down the stairs back into the kitchen.

Eleven

It was my idea to bring the chicken soup to Mary's. More than three weeks had gone by, and I hadn't seen her once. Robert had gotten the chicken pox after Eliza Ann, and then Randolf and Cyrus had gotten sick. Now, Mary herself was feeling poorly.

School was closed because of the summer heat, so Lydia was back home taking care of Mama. She was trying to make the house cheerful, but there was no little boy running around the kitchen, chasing me everywhere, wanting me to draw pictures for him. And there was no Mary, baking special treats and furrowing her brows and really listening whenever I talked with her. The whole house felt bigger and very empty without Mary.

"Can I, Mama? Can I bring them some soup? Lydia made a whole kettle. I've already had chicken pox . . . and if Mary is sick, too, it will be hard for her to cook for her family."

"That's a thoughtful idea, Phebe. But does thy sister need thee?"

"She's gone to the mill. She told me to sweep and sand the kitchen floor, but I've already done that, and I'll hurry back."

Mama looked toward the window. It was a gray, misty day.

"Wear thy cloak," she said. "And be careful not to spill any soup as thee goes."

I kept the heavy, warm soup pot pressed close to my body. Slosh. Slosh. The chicken soup rose to the sides of the pot like ocean waves as I walked. I held the pot firmly by the handles. The soup moved less that way. Why was that so? I wished that I could learn the why of things in school, rather than just learning facts and memorizing Bible passages.

Reading and writing weren't getting any easier, even though some of the letters were starting to make sense, now that Lydia had helped me every day when we'd been at school. But I still couldn't put them together.

I climbed the steep little hill to New Guinea. New Guinea: that's what people called the neighborhood where the Negro people lived. Once, when I'd been younger, I'd asked Papa, "If the light of God is in all of us, in every single person, why do the people from Africa have to live in a different place?"

Papa had sighed. "Thee does get to the heart of the question, doesn't thee, my little daughter." He'd picked me up and placed me on his lap. "I don't think it's right that they should. I think that we should all live together. But in this world, some people, and I'm ashamed to say it's our white brethren, some people see the light of God shining brighter in some people than in others."

The fog was thick in New Guinea, and especially so on

the whole of Angola Street. Mary's cottage was quiet and dark. From the other houses, I could see lanterns glowing dimly from behind small windows. But from Mary's house? Nothing. I knocked at the front door. No answer.

Had they run away? Was the chicken pox an excuse? Had they lied to us about the chicken pox and run away to Canada? Did they not even trust us?

I raced around the house to get to the side door, the soup sloshing up and out of the kettle.

"Mary! Mary!" I pounded on the door.

It opened. It was Arthur. He looked tired. "Phebe, what's wrong?"

"I . . . I thought . . . oh, I'm sorry. I . . . I brought thee some chicken soup." I held the pot out to him. "I'm sorry, I spilled some of it and it's wet on the side."

Arthur opened the door wide. "Come in, Phebe. This is very kind of you." He smiled. "Chicken soup for the chicken poxed." He laughed at this own joke.

"Arthur. What is it?" It was Mary calling from the front of the house. "Who is there? Who has come?"

"It's all right, Mary. It's Phebe. Everything's all right. Go back to sleep."

He lifted the heavy pot from my arms and placed it gently on the hearth. "Come in, now, Phebe," he said. "Come warm yourself by the fire. Here, give me your cloak, and I'll dry it on this rack."

"I spilled some soup on it. I'm sorry, I–"

"Now, let's have no more apologies," Arthur said.

"You have done us a great kindness. I was wondering what I was going to cook for tonight's meal, and now God, through you, has provided."

"Is everyone sick?" I asked.

"The boys are much better. Eliza Ann is taking care of them."

"And Mary? Does she have the chicken pox, too?"

"No, my young friend. Mary is feeling poorly in her spirit."

"Just like Mama," I said.

"What's wrong with your mama?" Mary asked. She was standing in the doorway, leaning against the frame. She looked limp and old, like my favorite rag doll, like she didn't have many bones left in her body. Her sleeping gown was dirty.

"Mary!" Arthur helped her come over to a chair by the fire.

"What's wrong with your mama?" Mary asked again.

"She isn't sitting up anymore," I said.

"That may be best, Phebe. Dr. Stackpole may be right."

"But . . . she's talking about dying." And then my tears came, rolling down from my eyes like the steady summer rain. "She needs thee, Mary."

"Me? She needs me?" Mary's mouth opened wide in surprise. "What can I do for your mama?"

"When thee were taking care of her, she was better. She smiled and laughed, and . . ." I wiped the tears from my face. "I'm sorry," I said. How could I be so stupid?

Here, Arthur and Mary were worried about the slave catchers, about horrible men coming to take Arthur back, and I was talking, crying even, about Mama. "I should go home. Mama told me to hurry home."

Arthur lifted my cloak off the rack and placed it gently over my shoulders. He squeezed me a little.

"Don't worry, Miss Phebe," he said. "God will provide. Your mother is a good woman, and Mary tells me she is strong."

"And I will be at your home tomorrow morning," Mary said.

I gasped, my hands flying up to cover my mouth. Arthur knelt down beside her and took her hand.

"You're right, Arthur," Mary said. "I have been feeling poorly in spirit. I have been crying and fretting and worrying only of our own troubles, and I have forgotten that other people need me. Just because I am afraid doesn't mean that I can stop being an instrument of God's will. I'll be there tomorrow morning, Phebe. Thank you for coming."

Twelve

It was three weeks later, and June had become July. Mary had come back, and even though Mama wasn't sitting up yet, she seemed happier. That afternoon, I had left Lydia at school after our reading time and gone to help Papa at his store.

"Does thee want me to place the new shoes on this shelf, Papa?"

"Just four or five pairs, Phebe," he answered. "Put the extras in the back room in the storage chest."

I loved the smell of the new shoes and the feel of the soft leather against my fingers. I placed my hand inside a shoe and pretended that it was a puppet.

"Hello, Phebe," it said.

"Hello, shoe."

But then, there was noise at the store entryway, and Lydia was running full speed through the door. "Slave catchers! Slave catchers are here! Gilbert Coffin . . . he . . . he says they're after Arthur." Lydia bent over, gasping for air. "Papa. Slave catchers. They're here."

Papa dropped the sack of coffee beans he was carrying. "Where? When?"

"On the *Hero*. Just docking."

"All right. Now, girls, no more running. Someone told

them that Arthur is here in Nantucket, and we don't want to attract any more attention. Lydia, take care of the store. Phebe, go home and tell Mary to stay in the house. I'm going to find Arthur."

"But Papa. Mary will want to–"

"She could lead them to him. Stay in the house."

I didn't run, but I walked as fast as my legs could move. Arthur was in danger. Arthur could be taken back. Every ounce of my strength had to go into walking as fast as I could to save Arthur. All of a sudden, someone's arms were around me.

"Phebe, what's wrong?" It was Richard Bunker, the stonemason who had built our kitchen garden stone wall.

"Nothing. I . . . I'm just . . . ."

"Something's wrong."

"No, I . . . ." Richard Bunker was staring at me with wide-open, honest eyes. At least, I had always trusted those eyes before.

"Please let me go. Please."

"All right, child. God speed you on your way. Do you need help? Can I–"

But I was already past the Pacific Bank and was running toward home.

"Mary!"

Mary was coming out the back door carrying a bucket of dirty water.

"Mary. Get back in the house. Quickly."

Mary froze.

"Quickly. Please, Mary."

"What's wrong, Phebe?"

"Slave catchers. They're here."

Mary dropped the bucket and started running toward the front.

"Mary, no. Thee has to stay." I grabbed at her waist, my arms reaching around, holding her tight. I felt the warmth of her, the power. But she was so strong. She kept moving forward, pulling me along like a sack of potatoes.

I wasn't going to be able to stop her. She was already dragging me along the side of the house, and we were almost to the street.

"Mary, thee will be seen. Thee will lead them to Arthur. Please, Mary."

"They'll hurt him. They'll kill him."

"Mary, please."

Mary began to scream a high-pitched, wordless scream as she twisted and turned and then tried to peel me off. "No, Mary, be quiet." When Mary loosened one arm, I held on tighter with the other. "Mary, stop screaming. People will hear. Please stop." I wouldn't let go of her for anything. I'd hold on forever if I had to, to keep Mary from running into the street.

Suddenly, we were looking into each other's faces.

"Thee could lead the slave catchers to him," I said. "Papa will find him. I promise."

"But the children. I have to find my children."

"Gilbert Coffin knows. He'll get them."

Mary went limp. "The children," she said. "Arthur."

"Come. Quickly." I pulled her up the stairs, and then Mary followed me down the hallway to the kitchen.

"Where should we hide?"

"The cellar," Mary said.

We ran down the steps. "Hide in the root cellar," I said, "just in case they come here and I can't keep them out of the house."

Mary, calm now, showing no emotion at all, pulled four sacks of carrots away from the corner and slipped silently behind them. She crouched down, holding herself tightly.

*　　*　　*

I was back upstairs in the kitchen.

"Phebe."

It was Mama, calling from her bed. I ran up the stairs.

"Phebe. Why was Mary screaming?"

"Slave catchers. Slave catchers are here, Mama. On the *Hero*. Just docking. Papa's looking for Arthur, and he told me to make Mary stay in the house. She's in the root cellar."

"Oh no. Poor Mary. And Arthur. I pray that Papa finds him." Then Mama half sat up and flung her pillow across the room. "It makes me so angry. Here I am stuck in this bed, and I can't do anything to help Arthur and Mary. I can't do anything. I'm worthless. I'm worth nothing. I–"

"Thee is worth everything to me, Mama."

She stared at me. "Come here, Phebe," she said. "Come. Come here. I'm sorry. Don't cry. I'll be fine."

She touched my tears, tracing the paths of them.

I closed my eyes and felt the quiet, gentle movement of her fingers on my face. Even though Mama was sick in bed, even though she couldn't do any of the normal things anymore, I needed her so much. Somehow, when Mama touched my face, I had hope that, someday, things would get better.

* * *

I sat in the front room and waited, listening to carriage wheels on the road and dogs barking. The wind teased tree limbs here and there. My whole body felt hurt and exhausted. Had I broken something in the struggle with Mary?

I tried to calm down so I'd look normal. I took long, deep breaths from the bottom of my stomach. Breathe in, breathe out. Feel the air come into my body. If the slave catchers came to our house, I'd tell them that Arthur and Mary had gone away somewhere, that they'd been gone for a week, that they probably went to Canada. I'd lie to them, I wouldn't care. God would want me to lie to them.

But there was a sound. Was it them? Was it . . . oh, thank goodness. It was Papa.

"Mary?" he asked.

"In the root cellar."

"That's my smart girl." He cupped my face in his big callused hands. "Go tell Thomas Mitchell what's happening. Tell him to meet me at the Meeting House just after dark. Don't run in the streets. We don't want to attract any more attention than we have to. Just walk quickly and deliver the message."

"But, did thee find him?" Is Arthur all right?"

"Yes. I'll go down right now and tell Mary that Arthur is safely hidden. And the children. She'll stay in the cellar till nightfall, and then we'll move her to a safer place."

Thirteen

"I'm so cold," Mary said. She was still huddled in the corner behind the carrots.

"Here." I held out the dark brown cloak. "Papa said to wear this tonight when thee travels to the Gardners'. Thee might as well put it on now."

Mary did not uncurl from her crouch.

I tried to ease her away from the cold rock wall and to place the cloak around her shoulders, but she was limp, leaden weight. As I touched her arm trying to move her, I realized that she was freezing.

"Mary, please, put this over thee. I'm going to go upstairs and get thee some hot soup."

"No, don't leave. Not yet, I . . ." She took the cloak, bunched it into a large mass, and hung onto it tight.

"The children are all in hiding, Mary. Randolf and Cyrus are in the Folgers' attic, and Eliza Ann and Robert are with Anna Macy."

"But they're not with their father. They need their father, they . . ." Her voice broke.

"Thee will join him tonight, at the Gardners'."

"But the children . . . ."

"Cyrus was afraid at first, but then he said that he was going to be brave for Randolf. And Anna Macy has a room on the second floor. It's in the back of the house and Papa says it's safe."

"But Robert's a baby."

"Anna Macy is cooking all his favorite things. She gave him toast and jam this afternoon. Blueberry."

"Robert loves blueberry." Mary loosened her grip on the cloak.

"Anna Macy says that she's going to make pies for tomorrow. Apple and pumpkin."

Mary almost smiled. "That is kind of her."

"She thinks the world of thee, Mary. She *wants* to take care of thy children."

Silence. A tear fell from Mary's eye, and then another. She wiped her face. "I'm sorry about before," she said. "I must have hurt you."

"I shouldn't have run up like that. I should have told thee different. Slower."

"No, it was my fault. I was . . . do you know what those men are doing?"

"They're walking around town, looking at all the houses. They went to Angola Street."

"To our house?"

"Past it. But they've done that everywhere." I sat down next to Mary.

"Anger grows in that kind of man," she said. "David Ricketts wants revenge on Arthur for getting away. They turned the countryside inside out looking for him." Mary's body began shaking. "At first, a friend took him to the swamp. Snakes," Mary said. "He almost went crazy with the snakes. A friend came and got him in three days and took him to his grandmother's."

"Too bad he didn't have a place like this to hide," I said. "Arthur could have stretched out and walked back and forth."

"But that's why it worked," Mary said. "It looked so small, and they came back to search again and again. Arthur heard them looking in the house, breaking his grandmother's things."

"He must have been so afraid."

"Especially for his grandmother. If they had found him. . . ."

"Did they ever find out? Later, I mean."

"We don't think so. And I don't know how they could have once Arthur was on that good Quaker ship." Mary placed the cloak over her shoulders. "But we've had no news, all these years. And his grandmother doesn't know that Arthur made it here and married me and that he has four children." She patted her stomach. "And a fifth on the way."

"We could write her. I mean, Lydia could. We could ask one of the Elders . . . sometimes Elders from Boston or Philadelphia visit, and they could take the letter and mail it from there."

"We could all write a part of it," Mary said. "Arthur, and Eliza Ann and the boys. Robert's too little, but he could tell me what to write. And you could write and tell her about yourself. Because you're a friend."

"Well, I . . . I'll do that," I said. And then I felt sick to my stomach. Here I was lying to Mary. I couldn't write a letter. I could barely write my own name.

"I feel stronger," Mary said. "I am so grateful that we've had warning and that your father has found Arthur."

"And the children are all safe," I said.

"Robert will be frightened," Mary said.

"I'll try to see him, to tell him that everything will be all right."

"Tell him to be a good boy," Mary said. "And to mind his manners and obey Anna Macy. Tell him that if I don't hear good of him, he will have to answer to me when we're back home."

"Those slave catchers can't stay here forever," I said. "They'll give up and go away."

Mary was silent. We listened to water dripping somewhere in the cellar.

"Mary, I'm going to bring thee something to eat. Lydia made clam chowder."

"I couldn't."

"It's good to keep thy strength up. And thee has to eat for the new baby."

Mary smiled. "I'll try to eat some," she finally said. "For the new baby. And for you."

Fourteen

I fell into a deep, exhausted sleep once Papa stopped in my room and told me that Mary was safely in hiding, and no one woke me on Saturday morning. When I finally got downstairs, Lydia was cooking in the kitchen. She handed me a bowl of corn porridge.

"Has thee been in the Gardners' attic?" I asked.

"No," Lydia said. "But Papa says they have a good room fixed up." Lydia sat down beside me, heavy, like a tired old woman. "Mama's upset," she said. "She wouldn't eat her breakfast. She said that God shouldn't have created a world where there was so much evil."

"Mama's right."

"This morning, Papa was talking about spiriting Arthur and the family off-island to Canada, giving them some money to get started again."

"No."

"He has to consider it, Phebe. It may not be safe for them here."

"They'd leave? They'd go to Canada?" I pushed my bowl of porridge away. We might never see each other again, not even be able to say good-bye, just like Arthur and his grandmother.

Lydia got up slowly, like she weighed as much as the

gristmill stone. "Remember when I didn't like Mary?" she asked.

I nodded.

"And here I am today, praying that she'll be able to stay."

*   *   *

The waiting took forever. There was a mid-August hot spell, and I knew it would be uncomfortable in the attic. I wanted to visit, but going there could endanger them. And I really wanted to see Robert and Eliza Ann, to tell them that everything would be all right. But Papa said that, it too, could be dangerous. I didn't normally go to visit Anna Macy, and Papa said that we should only do "normal" things. Village eyes were watching us.

The two slave catchers did nothing. Just stayed at the inn and took long walks about the island. It was as if they were waiting.

One day, they came into Papa's store. The tall one was shiny clean and all dressed up in a white shirt, blue waistcoat and trousers. His top hat was brown beaver felt. The fat one with the white whiskers was dressed like a farmer with a tan smock over trousers. He had a big mole on his left cheek. I memorized everything about them, I hated them so much.

"I'll have a box of your Havana cigars," the tall one said. "And may I buy a piece of that black licorice for your pretty daughter?"

"Thee can certainly buy the cigars, sir. Here they are." Papa took the money.

The fat one smiled at me. "But wouldn't your little daughter like a piece of that candy?"

"Phebe, go into the storage room and start unpacking that embroidery floss that arrived this morning."

"Yes, Papa."

"And I thank thee, sirs, for the offer, but I do not wish that my daughter should accept gifts from strangers."

"We meant no offense, sir. We were just trying to be friendly."

"No offense was taken," Papa said, "and I hope that thee both enjoy the cigars. Now, Phebe, go get that thread ready."

"Yes, Papa."

"Thank you, sir," the tall one said. "I'm sure that we will be back for more cigars." They turned and walked slowly out of the store.

"Go to the back, Phebe. Now."

I sat on a barrel of molasses and waited, holding my hands tightly together. Ten minutes later, he joined me.

"There is no embroidery thread back here," I said.

He sighed. "I know. It was the first thing I could think of."

"Papa, why was thee so polite to them?"

"They're fishing around, looking for anyone who looks nervous or angry. I want them to think that we have no feelings about Arthur and Mary."

"They have to know that Mary worked for us."

"Yes, that is why I was especially careful."

"But, Papa, then why didn't thee let them buy me the licorice?"

He reached over and touched my face. "I probably should have, but . . . there are limits. I just couldn't."

"And I wouldn't have been able to eat it," I said. "If I had to, for Arthur and Mary, I would have put it in my mouth and chewed, but I wouldn't have been able to swallow. I couldn't, Papa."

"I know, Phebe. There are just some things that we cannot swallow."

"But, Papa, how can they do it? How can they steal other people? Take them back to where they can be whipped and torn apart by hound dogs?"

"And separated from their families without thought, their labor stolen from them, their lives . . . Phebe, they do it for the money."

"The Elders are right, Papa. Money can make people evil."

Fifteen

"Mama, does thee want to turn on thy other side?" I asked.

"No, I'll just rest here awhile."

"We could talk, and I could . . . ."

"I'm tired, Phebe. I want to sleep."

"Does thee want me to open the window? There's a nice ocean breeze."

No answer. I opened the window halfway, resting it down on the thin piece of wood that was lying on the sill. The window made a creaking sound, and Mama groaned. But the breeze was pleasant. Maybe that would cheer Mama up.

"Would thee like something to eat? Lydia made an apple pie. It's delicious, and I could bring thee up a little piece, or a bigger piece if thee likes, and—"

"Phebe."

"What?"

"Please be quiet."

I sat on the little chair next to the cedar box. Finally, I reached down into my bag and took out my knitting. "It's a pretty day, Mama."

"Good."

As I pulled the chair closer to the light of the window,

the chair legs made a scraping sound against the floor. Mama twisted and groaned again.

"Is thee all right?"

"I'm fine." Mama's voice was so weak.

I went back to my knitting. Click. Click. The needles seemed big and bulky today, but still my stitches were nice and even. Click. Click. Click. Click.

"Phebe."

"What, Mama? Can I get thee something?"

"I'm trying to rest."

"What's the matter?"

"The needles. They're clicking."

"I'm sorry. I'll try to be quiet."

"Go downstairs and knit in the parlor."

"I want to be with thee."

All of a sudden, Mama's voice wasn't so weak anymore. "Just leave me alone," she said. "Leave me alone."

How could Mama say that to me? My needles clattered to the floor as I jumped. "Thee rested all morning, the whole day when I was at school. Thee is not even trying to get better. Thee doesn't even care about me. Why doesn't thee just die?" My hands flew up to cover my mouth, the mouth that had said such hateful things.

Mama was half sitting now, her eyes angry. She pointed her whole arm toward the stairway. "Get out," she said, not loudly. That almost made it worse. "Get out."

* * *

I was lying on my bed when Lydia came in. She sat

next to me and began stroking my hair. "I heard," she said. "I was walking up the stairs."

"Is thee going to tell Papa?"

"No."

"How could I have said such things to her?"

"Don't worry about that now," Lydia said.

"But she isn't trying. She has given up."

"I know."

Now the tears came. If Lydia had yelled at me, I never would have cried. "I said such awful things. I told Mama I wanted her to die."

"Thee didn't say that."

"I yelled at her."

"When I first heard, I started running. I was going to make thee stop. But then, then I heard thee say things that were true for me, too."

"Mama doesn't love us anymore."

"It's not true," Lydia said.

"I want Mary back. Mama is always better when Mary is here."

"I know. Mama still loves us, I think. But she's given up on the world, and she's given up on herself. Mama isn't trying to get better. She's just given up."

Sixteen

One September morning, the slave catchers quietly left Nantucket. On September 10, 1822, they boarded the *Loper* and were gone.

It took two weeks for Mary not to jump whenever someone came unexpectedly into the kitchen. And Robert just wanted to stay on my lap whenever he was over. Eliza Ann was the only one who seemed the same as before.

That afternoon, I had just put Robert down in the kindling box for his nap. "He's getting too big," I said. "We're going to have to get him a bigger bed."

Mary broke one egg and then another into the mixing bowl.

"Mary, can I help thee make the pudding?" I asked.

"No, child. You're always helping. Why don't you go visit Miriam Gardner and see if she wants to go outside with you. It's a fine fall day."

"Go to Miriam's?"

"She's a nice girl."

"We used to play sometimes, before Mama got sick."

"Go on, now. Take that pretty bird nest you found last week."

"What's Eliza Ann doing?"

"Cleaning for Mistress Folger."

"Oh."

I watched Mary whisk the eggs. The vanilla smell filled the kitchen. "But ..." Well, I couldn't go up to see Mama. Mama didn't want me. And it seemed as if Mary didn't want me, either.

But Mary was smiling. "Go on, now. You work too hard for a little girl."

Little girl. I wasn't a little girl. But I wouldn't stay where I was not wanted. I went upstairs to my room and shut the door.

*   *   *

Later, as I was heading out of my room to go to find Eliza Ann, I noticed that Mama's door was half open. Something made me stop in the hallway and stand close to the wall to listen.

"How did it hurt?" Mary was asking Mama. "When you first got hurt?"

"At first, it just hurt every way I lay," Mama said. "But there were no shooting pains. I was just so uncomfortable. And I couldn't sleep, and then I got more and more tired."

I heard the bed creaking.

"But tell me again what Arthur's grandmother did," Mama said.

"She rubbed his muscles, gently at first, and then she helped him walk a little. The first time he put weight on his legs, he fell to the floor."

"That was just from lying down?"

"On his back in that tiny space."

"I hate to think of him being in there all those months," Mama said. "It really was that small?"

"No more than four feet long and three feet wide and three feet at the highest peak. That's what kept him safe. They never thought so small a space could hide a person."

"We shouldn't be talking about this. It must be painful for thee."

"It's a relief to talk about it. I can't at home. I think we should leave Nantucket. Lord knows, I don't want to, but . . . for our children. But Arthur says that he won't run away again, that he'll fight this time."

"He is so brave."

"Brave and stupid. How can a slave fight? The laws are against him."

"That depends on who determines the law. And thee has friends."

"I know."

Silence. I watched a patch of sunlight form on the hallway floor as the sun came out. I knew that I should go, that I should move out into the middle of the hallway and walk quickly past Mama's bedroom and down the stairs. But some urgency in their voices kept me tight against the wall.

"These past weeks, since the slave catchers came, I lie in bed at night and pray that God will let us die in our sleep before the morning," Mary said. "All of us: Arthur, me and the children. I know I'm not supposed to, but . . .

I just believe in my heart that those slave catchers will be back."

"Thee doesn't know if thee can go on," Mama answered. "God will forgive thee for that wish."

She said it so kindly, like she really understood. Did Mama feel that way herself? Did she sometimes ask God to let her die in the night?

"Then Mary's voice became softer, and I strained to hear. I leaned forward, but then moved back. What if they saw me?

"Would thee rub my muscles, Mary?" Mama suddenly asked. "I know it's unfair to ask."

"You mean, like Arthur's grandmother?"

"Yes."

I held my breath.

"It frightens me. You were injured. You might get worse."

"I couldn't be worse. My little daughter has to tell me the truth, that I've given up? No, Mary. I've plenty of time to sit in the quiet and wait for the light to come these last few days. I've got to do something. If thee is willing, we should start. We should start slowly, but we should start."

"It could make you worse."

"I can't stay in this bed forever," Mama said. "I'll die."

I felt sick to my stomach. I felt like running into the room and screaming at Mama, screaming that she couldn't leave me, that she couldn't die.

"I know that it's unfair to ask thee," Mama said, "with thee being so worried."

"No," Mary answered. "It will not be a burden. It will help me to think less about my own troubles. I will be glad to try to help you. And if it's God's will, you'll get better."

Seventeen

It was a beautiful October day, one of those rare autumn days that was sunny and hot. Mama and Mary were both being good to me again, but they weren't saying anything about the back rubbing. And, as the weeks went by, it got harder and harder to ask.

"I'll race you to the corner," Eliza Ann said.

"It's too hot." I wiped the sweat off my face. Eliza Ann was so lucky. She could wear a short-sleeve dress with a hem that fell at her knees. And she was barefoot.

"I like thy dress," I said.

She held out her skirt for me to feel the fabric. It was soft, a tan color, with thin stripes of yellow and gold.

"It was Mother's dress," she said. "She cut it down for me."

"Can I see the locket?"

Eliza Ann reached around in back of her neck and unclasped the chain. I held the tiny pink heart up to the October sun and watched it sparkle tiny spots of light. "Thy father gave this to thee?"

Eliza Ann nodded. "When I was born. He says that I had stolen his heart, so he gave me a little piece of it to wear around my neck."

"My Papa never gives me things like this."

"Quakers don't believe in pretty things."

"Only pretty things that God makes." I kicked at a small stone in the road. "Does thee want to know a secret?"

Eliza Ann stopped and looked at me. "Do I have ears to hear it?"

"Sometimes, I wish I wasn't a Quaker. Sometimes, I wish I was a Methodist, like thee."

"Zion Methodist, Zion Methodist, that's our official name." She laughed. "It makes my tongue tired to say it. But your papa gave you the diary."

"So I would write in it."

"He said you could draw pictures."

"He'd rather have me write."

"I know," Eliza Ann sighed. "Do you want me to carry the basket?"

"I wish I could write."

"Do you want me to show you? My father taught me."

I shrugged. "Lydia says there's a patch of raspberries on the north side of Folger's Marsh." We'd finally reached the edge of town. I pulled the heavy wooden latch up from the gate and let Eliza Ann through.

"I don't want to pick raspberries," she said. "I want to go see the blackfish whales beached at Quidnet."

I went through the gate myself and dropped the heavy latch back down. It made a thud. "We're supposed to be picking berries for jam."

"They won't know. We can tell them the birds got the berries. It won't be a whole lie. The birds got some of the berries. Father says that nine blackfish whales beached this morning. They'll be taken away by this afternoon, so we have to go now."

"Blackfish whales are little whales," I said.

"Come on, Phebe. Let's just say we kept looking for berries, and then we got lost. We can walk fast. Besides, we have to take the Polpis Road, and that goes right by Folger's, so we can get the berries on the way back."

I stood and looked over the lowland below us. We were on a rise, and we could see the ocean on the far horizon. I loved this island, my island, where I could climb a little hill and look out for miles until my eyes found the sea. All the paintings of the mainland showed meadows and trees, forests of trees, trees everywhere with their big leafy branches that blocked the view. I wanted my eyes to wander on the gray and purple heathlands, to count shrub oaks and little ponds, and then to finally rest on the open ocean.

A good breeze had come up, and I was glad of my long sleeves and heavy dress. It would be fun to go see the blackfish, and it wouldn't take that long to get to Quidnet. Last May, blackfish had beached at Siasconset, and Peter Coffin and Richard Starbuck told us at school how they had jumped up on the bodies, all jumbled together on the beach.

"If we have time, we can go to Sesachacha Pond and put our feet in the water. Come on, Phebe. No one will ever know."

"I don't want to lie." But my feet were hot. It would be wonderful to take off my shoes and stockings and wade in the pond. I hiked up my skirts and felt the breeze blowing the heat from my body. It would be wonderful to go close to the ocean and to listen to the waves coming home to the shore. "Let's go," I said. "We'll pick raspberries on the way home."

* * *

The blackfish whales were all lined up: big, silent, dark bodies. Eliza Ann and I stood quiet, not wanting to go near.

"Peter and Richard stood on them?" Eliza Ann said.

"They said they did."

"I don't want to."

In the distance, we could hear carriages coming toward us, carriages carrying men who would cut up the meat and bring it back to town.

"They used to be alive. Free in the water and alive."

Eliza Ann and I turned quietly and started walking home.

Eighteen

We were back at school and, day after day, Lydia made me stay and work with her in the late afternoons. But, today, I really wanted to get home to see Mary. I was going to ask her, just ask her plain and simple, if she was rubbing Mama's back. I had to know if Mama was getting better. All of the other days this week, Mary had been gone by the time I'd gotten home.

"I'm tired," I said. "Can't we do this tomorrow?"

"We should have practiced more this summer," Lydia said. "And, yes, we will work tomorrow. And today. Thee is beginning to remember the letters."

I sighed and got up to get the water pail.

"Sit down."

"I'm thirsty." I lifted the ladle to my lips and drank a long thin swallow. "The ladle is greasy," I said. "I'll go wipe it off."

"Sit," Lydia said. "The ladle can be greasy for another few minutes."

"But I want. . . ."

"What?"

"To go home." Should I tell Lydia? That I wanted to see if Mary was really rubbing Mama's back? "Mama said. . . ."

"Mama said what?"

"That she wants me to come home early."

"Why?"

"To sit with her, to do some knitting in her bedroom. Mama says she's lonely."

Lydia took the water pail and ladle from me. "It is greasy."

"I told thee."

"But it's not that bad." Lydia drank a whole ladle. "Mama has been lonely," she said, "ever since Dr. Stackpole made Anna Macy stop visiting."

"At least he doesn't know about Mary."

"What about Mary?"

"Just that she's there."

"He knows that Mary's there."

"I know, but . . . ." This lying was so hard. Maybe I should just tell Lydia what I'd overheard in the hallway all those weeks ago.

"Just go," Lydia said. "I can tell that thee wants to get home to Mama. And if Mama asked thee, go home."

I should have been happy, but I almost felt like crying. Lydia didn't even suspect that I had lied.

*   *   *

But I was on my way early, and as soon as I got outside into the open air, I breathed the autumn freshness into my body and felt better. The trees along Front Street were well turned to orange and yellow, and I kicked at some brilliant leaves at my feet. If we could like things that God made, why couldn't we like pretty things that men made, like the beautiful locket that

Arthur had given Eliza Ann? Didn't God help men make those things? I'd have to ask Papa.

*   *   *

I pushed open the door, hoping to find Mary in the kitchen. I was just going to ask her, plain and simple. I was just going to tell her what I'd heard.

Mary wasn't in the kitchen. "Slowly, now," I heard her say, as I climbed to Mama's bedroom. "Here, lean on me and go slowly now."

"What was happening?" I raced up the stairs.

Mama was standing up! Standing up by the fireplace, leaning on Mary. "Phebe!"

"Mama!" I couldn't move. I couldn't breathe.

"It's all right," Mary said in a voice that sounded like it came from far away. "Your mother is all right. Here, let me help her come back to bed."

I watched as they moved in slow motion across the room. Mama was moving her legs in an awkward way, but she was walking.

Suddenly, all I cared about was that Mama was better. "Mama, thee can walk. It's so wonderful." I burst into tears.

They kept moving in slow motion until they reached the bedside, and then Mary gently helped her back onto the bed. And then, I heard the door slam downstairs. It was Lydia!

"Quick, Mama, get under the covers."

"Oh, Phebe." Mama sighed. "I don't know what to do."

"Lydia will tell Papa and they'll make thee stop."

Lydia was climbing the stairs.

"Please, Mama."

Mary pulled the blanket up and covered her.

"I don't know, Phebe. What am I teaching thee?"

"What's wrong, Phebe?" Lydia said. She was looking in the door. "Why is thee crying?"

"I . . . I don't know. I'm just tired."

Lydia stood there, watching the three of us.

"Go to thy room, Phebe." Mama finally said, "and try to sleep until supper."

Nineteen

Strangely, I did sleep, waking only to take a little meal, and then I went back to bed. I was awakened by noises in the middle of the night. I leaped out of bed, confused, afraid. What was wrong? Was it Arthur and Mary? Someone was banging on the door downstairs.

"Come! It's the Coopers. Slave catchers are here."

"Arthur and Mary!" Now I ran so fast my feet barely touched the stairs. I threw open the door to Mr. Washington, a man who herded sheep outside of the village.

"Get your father."

"I'm here, just slower than my daughter." Papa was behind me, his hair disheveled. "What's happening George? It's four in the morning."

"Slave catchers . . . three of them . . . Sheriff Griffiths from Virginia and two deputies. They're at the house, with guns. So far, the neighbors have kept them off, but they're banging on the door."

"Is the door holding?"

"So far. The crowd's made the sheriff cautious, at least when I was there."

"George, go tell Gilbert Coffin to meet me at the Coopers'. And, Phebe, go back to bed."

I stood frozen, undecided, but then raced after Papa,

who was already running up the stairs. But he was too fast for me, and was already in his room with the door shut, getting dressed. I clenched my fists and hurried down the hall and threw on my dress and shoes.

I stopped. Papa had told me to go back to bed. But I had to do something, I couldn't just stay here, not knowing what was happening. I waited for a few minutes so that Papa would get a head start, and then I moved.

Good thing Lydia and Mama were such heavy sleepers. I tiptoed past their bedrooms, and then I followed Papa into the cold October night.

*   *   *

There were loud, angry voices and the deep murmur of a large crowd as I neared Angola Street. So many people were carrying lanterns that it was light, almost like dawn. I stood off at a little distance and watched, not knowing what to do.

I edged my way along the outside of the crowd. There were a hundred people at least, standing close together in the street, all facing Arthur's house, all closely watching what was happening at the door. I recognized Arthur's friend Absalom Quarry, and the small, thin man who chopped wood for Mistress Macy. I saw a few women, and some boys older than me. All of them seemed joined together like a dark mass of seaweed, pressing forward with the waves. And they were angry.

"Devils, get out of here," Absalom shouted. "Go back to where you belong. There are no slaves here."

Arthur and Mary's neighbors were lifting their fists

and shouting. "Get out of here. Devil men." They were gathered together like storm clouds. The odd light of the lanterns made me think of the time just before a hurricane, when the air was tense and heavy, ready to erupt.

But thank God that the neighbors were here. They were the ones who had kept the off-island sheriff from breaking down the door. They were the ones who had run through the night for help. Some of them may have been slaves in the South. All of them knew how Arthur felt.

Staying to the edge of the crowd, I crept closer to the house until I could finally see the door. And there was Papa, standing in front of Mary's house, facing a man with a long, evil gun. The man was waving the gun in the air and shouting.

Someone strode past me. It was Gilbert Coffin. He was so close that his cloak brushed my dress, but he was so intent on weaving through the people to reach the house, he didn't notice me. I shrank back behind a bush.

The crowd was louder now. "Devils. Get out of here. Devils. Go back to where you belong. There's no one in there. It's an empty house. There are no slaves here on Nantucket."

Someone grabbed me from behind and held on to my waist, fingers pressing me tight. "It's not safe here, child. Go home." It was a tall, big man, one of Arthur's neighbors. His hands almost encircled the whole of me.

"But I've got to—"

"It's not safe here. You go home now. We'll take care

of this. No one will take Arthur and his family."

I stopped struggling. "Sir, I've got to give something very important to my father."

"Are you telling me a falsehood, child?"

The crowd was moving forward now, pressing closer to the off-island sheriff. The lanterns moved jaggedly as people raised their fists and shouted, "Devils. Get out of here."

Sheriff Griffiths shook his fist at the crowd. "Keep away."

"Go back where you belong," someone answered.

Papa raised both his arms high. "Friends, please," he shouted. "We must not have bloodshed. This man will leave with no prey, I promise thee."

There was a roar from the crowd, and Arthur's neighbor loosened his grasp. In that instant, I slithered out of his arms and ran blindly until I saw the little alleyway next to Mary's house. I ran down it to the back.

Twenty

There were two men standing at the back of the house: burly, menacing shadows. As I strained to see, my eyes finally adjusted to the deeper darkness. The men were white, strangers, the deputies. They were not the same slave catchers who had come to our island before.

I crouched down behind a juniper and watched the men standing quietly, smoking cigars. Did Mary and Arthur know they were there? The men were waiting to see if the family would try to escape by the window in the back.

How dare they stand so quietly! They didn't belong. They wanted to capture Arthur. I wanted to scream, to tell them to go away from there, but I kept the yells in my throat. Those men wouldn't listen to me, a little girl with little-girl screams.

One of the men picked up a rifle from the ground. The house was dark. I could feel its stillness, the huge weight of it leaning into the shouting in front. Mary and Arthur were probably hiding in the kitchen. And the children. Eliza Ann. Eliza Ann who wasn't afraid of anything.

My mouth was parched. I barely breathed.

Papa might not know that the deputies were in the back, and none of the neighbors were back here watching them. The deputies could decide to smash in

94

the window with their guns. I had to warn Papa. I edged my way toward the front of the house until I could hear Papa's voice above the angry murmurs of the crowd.

"We are not interfering in thy business, sir. We just wish to know what business thee has on our island at four o'clock in the morning." He sounded calm, but very sure, with that firm tone that he only used when he was very angry. I felt proud of him. Papa would not fight with a gun or with his fists, but he was fighting with words.

The crowd had grown quiet. They were listening to Papa, too.

"We have come for our property," Sheriff Griffiths said. "Stand aside and let us in."

"What property is it that thee has to wake up these good people from their beds?" Papa pointed to the crowd.

"Stand aside. I have a warrant. Look, sir, it is a warrant issued for Arthur Cooper, runaway slave from the plantation of David Ricketts, and for the wife and children of the slave."

No, it couldn't be. They were trying to take away Mary and the children! Robert! Cyrus! Randolf! Eliza Ann!

"There must be some mistake. Thee said thee has come for property. These are people thee speaks of, not property," Gilbert Coffin said.

"I am well aware of your abolitionist views. But you live in this country. You have to abide by the laws."

"I think the law would say, sir, that thee is creating a

disturbance, and that thee should leave this place at once. Come by our Magistrate's office in the morning, and he will discuss thy claim."

"You shelter slaves here," Sheriff Griffiths said. "It is well-known. If we leave, the slaves will be gone by morning."

The crowd was murmuring again. There was a *thud*. Stones were being thrown. And Papa and Gilbert Coffin were standing right next to the sheriff. They could be hurt.

The sheriff raised his gun and aimed it at the crowd. "Stand back."

"Friends. Please." Papa was raising his arms and yelling. "There is no Arthur Cooper here for this man to find. No wife and children. He will soon realize his error and leave of his own accord."

But the people kept shouting. I could feel the fury that was blinding their fear. Absalom Quarry and two other men started walking toward the sheriff. Absalom was carrying a long, heavy stick. "You'll go now," Absalom shouted. "Get out of here."

"Stand back or I'll shoot you," the sheriff yelled.

Papa stepped between Absalom and the sheriff. "Friends. Bloodshed will not help. It will only draw more sheriffs from off-island."

The crowd quieted. Then I heard a muffled cry from within the house. Robert! The sound only lasted a moment, and I held my fists tight to my mouth, praying that only I had heard it.

"I have a warrant," Sheriff Griffiths yelled.

"Let me see that so-called warrant," Papa said.

Sheriff Griffiths handed him a large sheet of paper.

"Look, Friend Coffin," Papa said. "Sheriff Griffiths says he has a warrant here for the return of a person named Arthur Cooper and for his wife and children. I think, perhaps, that the warrant might be a forgery. Let us examine it. Gilbert, kindly hold that light over here." Papa seemed to be reading the paper. But I knew what he was really doing. He was stalling for time. Time, I thought, he was stalling for time, until he could think of some way to save Arthur and Mary and the children.

Twenty-one

Oliver Gardner and Anna's brother-in-law Thomas Mackral Macy strode toward Papa, parting the crowd the way that boats pushed into the surf part the waves. The two Friends reached Papa. Now, at least, there were four of them facing the off-island sheriff.

Maybe one of them could get the deputies to come up front, and maybe then . . . . I had to reach Papa. I ran to him and pulled at the back of his cloak. He turned and crouched down, holding me tight.

"Phebe, go home. Go home now."

"Papa, there are two deputies in the back."

"I know, child. Go home. Go home now."

"But, if someone can get them to come up front . . . there's a window."

"They'll be seen."

"But if we do it before dawn . . . ."

Sheriff Griffiths was waving the warrant in the air and shouting at the crowd. Absalom Quarry was coming closer again, holding the stick aloft. He looked frightened this time, but determined. I saw two people bend down to get stones from the street.

Oliver Gardner raised his arms. "Friends, we will have the matter settled soon. Please be patient. I know that this gentleman will see fit to leave of his own accord."

Papa stared at me for a moment, looking hard at my face. Then he whispered. "We'll do it. We'll get them out the back. Go home, Phebe. It's not safe for thee here."

"But thee needs me. Mary will recognize my voice, and she'll open the window."

"No, I won't risk thee."

"Papa, I have to help."

"No."

"Please, Papa."

He hesitated. "If there is shooting, thee must promise me that thee will fall to the earth."

"I promise."

"Right away."

"I promise."

He finally nodded. "Yes," he said. "Go quietly." He rose and turned, shielding me from Sheriff Griffith's view.

I eased to the corner of the house and then dropped behind the juniper bush and worked my way to the back. The deputies were still standing like statues, moving only their arms up and down, up and down, lifting the cigars to their mouths. The breeze carried the cigar smoke to me, and it overcame me and made me want to gag. I held my breath.

Hours passed, it seemed. I stared at the men and then turned away, afraid that they might sense me watching them. I took deep breaths and counted them . . . twenty . . . twenty-one . . . twenty-two. What was Papa doing? Why wasn't anything happening? The first light of dawn was already touching the darkness. Then all of a sudden, I felt a man stride by toward the deputies.

"Mr. Bass. Mr. Taylor," Gilbert Coffin called. He was calling to the deputies. "The Magistrate is here. He wishes to examine thy papers."

"We are hired by Sheriff Griffiths," the tall man said. "Our papers are in order."

"Magistrate Folger needs to speak with thee," Gilbert Coffin said. "He does not think the warrant is legal in Massachusetts."

"It's a federal warrant," the short man said. "You have to abide by the law."

"Our Massachusetts law differs," Gilbert Coffin argued, "and we are in Massachusetts."

"You are wrong," the tall one said. But he left his post and began to walk toward the front of the house. The short man joined him.

Step. Step. Step. Step. Step. Step.

Then, Oliver Gardner was running from the other side of the house. I flew toward him and we reached the window together.

"Mary! Arthur! It's me. It's Phebe. Open up. Please." Silence.

"Mary, please. I have help."

The windowsill shuddered, and Oliver tore the window open and lifted me up so that I could climb through. Mary was sheltering the children in the corner. Arthur stood in front of them with an ax in his hands. As soon as he saw me, he dropped it on the floor.

Oliver threw his hat and cloak to Arthur. "Put these on," he said. "Quickly."

All of them seemed frozen. Mary stared at me with wide, terrified eyes. She looked huge, as though she was about to deliver the new baby any second. Then Robert began to cry, and Eliza Ann picked him up, and Arthur sprang into action.

"We'll walk, not run," Oliver said. "We'll go behind the houses to Pleasant and then to High. Follow me."

No one spoke. Arthur and Oliver Gardner helped all of us through the window. In silent file, we walked away from the house, listening to the crowd's angry shouts from the front. It was really lighter now, so we could see to step around the rocks and bushes in our path.

When we reached the large elm at the corner of Miller's Lane, Eliza Ann stepped aside and waited for me at the back of the line. She silently handed me her little brother.

Eliza Ann was amazing. I knew that she was terrified, she must have been terrified to have her own life and the lives of her family be so threatened. And yet, I truly believe that on that October morning, she gave me Robert to comfort *me*.

Somehow, Robert wasn't heavy at all. I held him close to me and for the first time felt my shivering start to calm. But it was still hard to walk slowly past all the houses down Pine Street, and over to School. Someone might be looking out. Was that a curtain pulled aside? A sliver of lantern light?

Most people in Nantucket would never tell. But someone had told Sheriff Griffiths where Arthur lived. That person could be watching us right now.

When we got to Main Street, Oliver Gardner stopped. "Go home, Phebe, I'll take the family to their hiding place, and they'll be safe there. And Sheriff Griffiths will find an empty house on Angola Street."

Mary reached for Robert. I wanted to say something to make the anguish leave her face. I wanted to tell her that they would be safe, that everything would be all right, that no one would ever threaten them again. But I could only give her back her little boy and then feel tears well up in my eyes.

Mary bent down and kissed me on my forehead. The group then turned and walked away.

Twenty-two

Even though I was exhausted, I couldn't go to bed. I sat in the kitchen remembering Mary. She was a ghost in the room: chopping onions, peeling potatoes, turning and laughing and handing me a piece of blackberry pie. I almost could smell the pungent aroma of Mary's braised meat stew.

Papa came home when the windows started to brighten, around six o'clock. "Let's take a walk," he said. He held open the door and we went out together.

I pulled my cloak tight around my body. It was foggy and damp, and the ocean breezes made me cold. When we finally reached Commercial Wharf, we stood and watched a group of sea gulls flying in circles up above and then settling back down onto the rocking water.

Papa did not speak for a long time.

"I'm sorry," I said. "Thee told me to stay home, and I went to Angola Street. I deserve to be punished."

Papa was still looking away. Maybe he would never forgive me. That would be worse than the most horrible punishment.

But then he stirred. "I don't know what to do," he said. He was looking out over the ocean, talking to himself. "Phebe disobeyed me, but she did so because she cared for Mary and her family. She risked her own safety because of the needs of others. Quakers do that, even Quaker children. I think about all the children in the South who are risking themselves for the Railroad."

"I'll never disobey thee again," I said.

"If Mary was in trouble and I said not to help her, thee would obey?"

"But that would never happen."

"It might, if I felt thee was in danger," Papa said. "And I did feel that last night, Phebe. Last night, there were guns and angry men, men who felt they had the power of the law, and a mob. It was not safe for a child."

"Or for thee, Papa. Thee put thyself in danger, too."

Papa sighed. "That is true, child. But I have lived more years and I make my own decisions about my safety. God has put thee in my care until thee is grown."

Papa was right. "I did not want to disobey thee," I said.

"I know that." He bent down and cupped my face in his cold, big hands. "And the other part is that I'm proud of thee. That thee cares for others, that thee is brave and quick-witted, even when there is danger."

I relaxed my tight fists. Everything was going to be all right. Papa did not hate me. Someday, he might even forgive me.

We stood and watched the early morning wharf. Men were starting to wash the deck of the *Industry*, getting it set to sail out next Thursday.

"Maybe we should . . . ."

"What, Phebe?"

I curled my toes in my shoes and pressed my lips

together. If I said it, Papa might agree. But it was right. "Maybe we should go to the Meeting House and sit and wait for God's light to tell us what my punishment should be."

Papa smiled. "Go to the Meeting House during the week? Sit in silence on a weekday? I know how hard First Day meetings are for thee, child." He took my hand and began to walk. "I think that sitting in silence is a punishment for thee. And, it also sounds like a good idea. We will sit together."

Twenty-three

We sat for hours, it seemed. My mind was busy and, for once, I did not try to stop the pictures: Mary shielding the children with her body, her jaw set firm and determined. Arthur facing the window with the ax. Eliza Ann handing me Robert and then taking her place in line and walking straight and tall. Mary, holding herself proud as she walked up Pine Street.

What would Mama do without Mary? Would she just give up like the first time when Mary had to be in hiding?

She couldn't. I wouldn't let her. Mama had walked, I had seen her. I would do what Mary had done. Mama would lean on me and I would help her practice when Papa was at the store and Lydia was at school. They didn't have to know.

Then, in my mind, I saw Cyrus: Cyrus who always had such a happy laugh, and then I saw Randolf, always so serious and polite. The slave catchers were trying to catch Cyrus and Randolf! If they could, they would take them both down South and make them be slaves.

No! I sat up fast, and Papa coughed. I'd never before sat next to Papa at the Meeting House. He was always on the facing bench, and I was with the women.

Papa. How could I not tell him about Mama? It was a kind of lie not to tell him.

Mary. Walking down Pine Street. Mama. Leaning on Mary. Eliza Ann. Robert. Arthur. I closed my eyes tight and tried to breathe deeply. "Please, God," I prayed. "Let Arthur and Mary be safe. Let Eliza Ann and Robert and Cyrus and Randolf and the new baby be safe. And, God, please help me to do the right thing about Mama."

* * *

My legs felt heavy as I walked up the stone steps to the kitchen. Papa and I had sat in silence for over three hours. Now, I was home and I knew what I had to do.

Lydia was already at school, and Papa had told me to have some breakfast and then to go to sleep for the morning. I took a loaf of bread from the shelf next to the fireplace, and put that and some jam on a tray. Mama might be hungry.

She was lying on her side facing the window.

"Mama, slave catchers–"

"I know, Phebe. Gilbert Coffin stopped by and told us this morning. And I know that thee has been sitting and praying with thy father."

I placed the tray on the cedar chest and sank down on my knees next to her bed. "Will Arthur and Mary be all right?" I asked.

"They're safe for now."

"Why was the warrant issued for all of them? Mary and the children were never slaves."

"I don't know. That's not legal, even by the laws of Virginia."

"But who could have done it? Who could have told?"

"I'm glad I don't know. It would be a terrible burden to still act kindly toward that person."

"I wouldn't. Why do we have to?" I stood and paced around the room. "I wouldn't."

"Remember, Phebe, most people are good. It must have been a sad, sorry soul who told Sheriff Griffiths where the Coopers live."

"But we got them away."

"Their brave neighbors faced men with guns and held them off."

"Can Arthur and Mary ever go back home to Angola Street?"

"I think so. Once Sheriff Griffiths leaves the island, I doubt he'll return. I think that the family will be able to stay here with us."

I sank down again next to Mama at her bedside. "Mama, thee has to let me help thee. I can do what Mary did. I can rub thy muscles and help thee to walk. Thee can tell me what to do, and I can–"

"Oh, my sweet daughter."

"We have to, thee can't give up. Thee has to be really walking by the time Mary gets out of hiding."

"I've been tired from the walking, but I've been all right. There have been no sharp pains. But Dr. Stackpole and thy Papa–"

"We have to tell them. We have to tell Papa and Lydia, and we have to tell them that it's working and they can't make us stop."

Mama turned her face away.

"They can't make thee stop. Thee is a strong woman. Mary said so."

"Mary said that?"

"Yes, to Arthur. Arthur told me when I brought them the chicken soup." I took a deep breath. "I have lied this year, and I would still lie for Arthur and Mary, like if the slave catchers asked me where they were hiding. But this is different. I . . . I don't want to lie anymore. I want to tell the truth and be strong, just like Arthur and Mary are, and Eliza Ann and . . . Eliza Ann was so brave this morning."

Mama sat up. She just sat straight up in bed. At that moment, I knew that she was going to be all right.

"I don't want to lie anymore, either, Phebe. I don't like hiding what I'm doing. Did Mary really say that I was strong?"

"Yes, that's what she told Arthur."

"Well, Mary is right about most things, so I have to prove her right about this. I think thee is right. I should be really walking by the time Mary gets out of hiding."

"Maybe thee can walk with me to Angola Street to welcome them home."

Mama laughed. "I don't know. We can try, but I'm going to at least be walking around our own house by that time."

I felt so happy, I couldn't stay still. I moved from one side of the room to the other, skipping and jumping as I went, and then I came over to Mama and kissed her face.

"Think about it, Phebe," Mama said. "Here, Mary and Arthur are forced to go into hiding for their lives, which is so unfair that they should have to suffer so. But even now Mary is helping me with the memory of her words. Sometimes I get selfish, and I think that God has sent Mary here to this house just to help me."

"It's just like what Mary says, Mama. She told me the next day after I brought her the chicken soup." I skipped around the room two more times, and then I bent over the tray on the cedar chest and sliced two thick pieces of bread and smothered them with jam. The jam reminded me of the first time I'd met Mary and Robert, when I'd washed his little fingers and we'd all become friends. I handed a slice of bread to Mama. "Mary says that all of us frightened people are sent to this Earth to help each other. And, now, I believe her."

Afterword

This is a fictional story based on a historical event. Arthur and his family were real people. Phebe and her family are fictional characters.

Arthur Cooper was born into slavery on October 1, 1789, on the plantation of David Ricketts in Virginia. Sometime before Arthur was nineteen years old, he escaped to the North, it is believed on the Quaker ship the *Regulator*. He settled in New Bedford, Massachusetts, and met Mary, a free-born person. They married in 1808 and had three children: Eliza Ann, Cyrus and Randolf. After Randolf was born in 1814, the family moved to Nantucket, where they had a fourth child, Robert.

In the early morning hours of October 24, 1822, Sheriff Griffiths and his deputies stood banging at the door of the escaped slave, Arthur Cooper. A crowd of neighbors gathered and kept the sheriff from entering the home until Quaker abolitionists came and further distracted the slave catchers.

Arthur and Mary and their four children escaped out of a window in the back and fled to the attic and cellar of Oliver Gardner. They were sheltered there and in other homes for several weeks, until Sheriff Griffiths finally gave up and left, never to return.

Mary delivered a fifth child on her fifth day of hiding.